SERPENT'S TONGUE

R.F. SHARP

ISBN: 0615868029
ISBN-13: 978-0615868028

First Edition

rfsharp@gmail.com

Website: http://www.rfsharpbooks.com

A New Sydney Simone Mystery/Suspense Novel
SERPENT'S TONGUE

MacGyver meets Dexter in the guise of Sydney Simone: skilled contract killer and righter of wrongs. When the system fails to provide justice, Sydney steps in--for a price.

The call for a contract hit on Earl the Cannibal came through Sydney's website, HumanPestControl.com. Taking out Earl, a child killer who had been wrongfully acquitted of horrific crimes was almost a public service—so she did it. But that wasn't the end. A week later she was called upon to eliminate a notorious con-man. Both hits fit her standards of bringing justice to those whom the system had failed. Apparent accidental death is Sydney's preferred method of killing, and the authorities buy that explanation—at first.

Sydney thinks her work is done, so she settles into her routine, running the Rose Madder Gallery with her partner/possible future husband, Oscar. But her life is soon turned upside down. The press ties both killings to the murder of a teenage boy. A police task force is created to track down what they call the Bible-Rose serial killer. Sydney is being framed and is not happy.

The first two killings were paid for by Pastor Luke Anger, a snake-handling revivalist preacher with nasty habits involving children. Convinced that Pastor Luke is using her as a serial-killer surrogate to cover up his own crime, Sydney must find a way to bring Luke to justice while keeping herself out of the eyes of the authorities. It's a fight or flight situation and Sydney is not about to flee.

R.F. Sharp

For Tarah and Elise
And of course Susannah

Also by R.F. Sharp

Fiction:
No Regrets, No Remorse

Non-fiction:
Winning the Divorce War
Living Trusts for Everyone

R.F. Sharp

SERPENT'S TONGUE
R.F. Sharp

"And these signs shall follow them that believe: In my name shall they cast out devils; they shall speak with new tongues. They shall take up serpents; and if they drink any deadly thing, it shall not hurt them; they shall lay hands on the sick, and they shall recover."

Mark 16:17-18

SERPENT'S TONGUE

The Job

Sydney followed Jude Ellis every day for three weeks before finding a way to murder him. Killing wasn't an easy thing for her to do. Not that she couldn't do it—she was willing enough—it was the method that was problematic. Shooting him would be easiest, she thought. But she didn't own and had never fired a gun of any kind. Plus she was only seventeen, living alone in her mother's apartment in Staten Island where guns weren't legally available; so where would she get one?

Running him down with a car would work if Sydney had a car or knew how to drive. She was average size for a girl but too small to beat him to death or try some kind of hand-to-hand killing with a knife or some other weapon. Other options like poisoning or blowing up his house were equally impractical since she hadn't yet learned those skills. So Sydney followed him every day without any sort of plan but felt like she was at least doing something. Being pro-active.

There was a lot of information about Ellis from the trial. He didn't take the stand in his own defense, but there were plenty of witnesses. Sydney and her mother attended every day; waiting to see what they were going to do to the man who abducted, raped, and killed Patrick, her twelve-year-old brother. Ellis was a thirty-two year old white male, a graduate of Mumford High School in Detroit before he migrated to New York.

Until he was caught for the murder he had worked as a route salesman for Empire Potato Chips. She imagined seeing him throwing bags of chips on the racks in the grocery. Tall and skinny with a pale complexion and acne he hadn't out-grown. After he was convicted and sent to prison he lost that job and they didn't give it back when he was released on appeal.

The news said that his trial suffered from what the appeals court called, "ineffective assistance of counsel". She interpreted that as meaning he had a shitty lawyer. Now he was back on the street like nothing had ever happened. The only job he could get after being released was as a kitchen worker in the Parthenon, a Greek breakfast and lunch place on the lower West side in Manhattan. Every day Sydney would walk past several times and look through the window.

He did the grunt work, cleaning up, emptying the garbage, mixing ten-gallon batches of salad dressing—stuff like that. He never looked up or out the window. The other workers talked, laughed, and seemed to be enjoying their work. But they didn't talk to him nor he to them. Maybe he was thinking about a new victim. She watched him as closely as possible without getting caught looking and knew his routine. The work didn't look hard. She wondered if he liked it better than working with potato chips.

To follow him Sydney had to get up early and take the train, then the subway. A subway station was near his house where she began her days of following and watching. She usually packed a lunch to save money. She staked him out from half a block away. Weird guys approached her from time to time but they left when she pretended to talk on her cell and refused to acknowledge them as a life form.

Sydney's mom had died right after Ellis was convicted but before he was released. Stress, they said. Sydney blamed Ellis for her death. Too much for her weak heart. Mom had suffered from heart problems for years and said her time was coming sometime soon but it was still a surprise. She died thinking the legal system had worked, but she left Sydney alone. So Sydney quit going to school. Eleventh grade wasn't so interesting anyway. She hung out in the apartment and stopped talking to her friends. Mom's aunt Lottie had taken care of the funeral arrangements.

There was a little money left in mom's checking account so Sydney forged her name on the rent checks and found three credit cards with practically no balances on them. These she used to transfer cash advances online to the checking account. The debit card was still working and Sydney got walking around money that way. But it was running out. She had been using one card to pay off the minimum each month on the others and was close to the credit limit on all of them now.

There were no other close relatives. Mom knew she was leaving Sydney in a fix and tried to smooth things for her. She pre-planned her burial and made arrangements for Sydney to go to Florida to live with Aunt Lottie when the time came. But she didn't go and Auntie didn't call back after Sydney said she was going to live with an aunt on her father's side. But her father was dead and had no sisters so that was a lie. She was Sydney Simone, her brother's sister, her mother's daughter, and she knew how to take care of herself.

After work, which was usually around three, Jude Ellis would walk directly to the subway. Once he stopped and bought a hot dog from a street vendor. Sydney thought that odd since he could have had all the hot dogs he wanted for free at work. He only put mustard on it. He never noticed her following, but that was probably because she didn't look the same as she had at his trial. She had sat in the front row every day for two weeks, right behind him, but he was facing toward the judge so it could be he had other things on his mind and didn't notice her at all.

When she heard on the news that Ellis was going to be released she called detective Ramirez, one of the cops originally assigned to the case. He was apologetic, as if he had to make excuses for the system. There was nothing that could be done, he said. They would keep an eye on him in case he did anything else. She was angry. Did that mean he had to kill someone else for justice to be served? The first killing was free? She hung up on him. There was only her to avenge Patrick.

After Ellis was released from prison Sydney cut her hair short and bleached it a dirty blond, not trying to look attractive. A disguise. Sydney was young but knew how to dress to either attract attention or not, so was pretty inconspicuous. Instead of a purse she always carried one of those cloth grocery bags. Kept her lunch and stuff in it. Including a boning knife from the kitchen. She had no plan but wanted to be ready for anything.

Ellis worked six days a week with Sundays off. There was a small park down the street from his house and on Sunday she would sit on a bench with a library book and watch for a few hours. Sometimes he never came out and she would go home. He didn't go to church, but then neither did she. Was she as bad as him, she wondered? She was determined to kill him. So they would both be killers.

Before her health deteriorated Sydney's mother would usually take Patrick and Sydney to Sunday school and church. The pastor preached loudly about going to hell, claiming that they were all sinners and their only hope to stay away from everlasting damnation was to repent. It scared her into repenting pretty often even though she couldn't figure out what she had done wrong. So would Ellis and she both go to hell? Would she see him there? No. There had to be a special place for someone like him. She planned to send him there, wherever that place turned out to be.

April 10, a Monday morning, Sydney was on time, waiting for him at the subway station. She was on the platform, back against the wall, knowing he would be coming down the stairs to the left. He always took the same train and always tried to sit in the front car. He even had a favorite seat, facing the doors. The car was never more than half full where they got on. She always worked her way to the second car where she could see him but he wouldn't notice her, just in case he got off at a different stop. He never did.

He came slouching down the steps on time, wearing his favorite Detroit Red Wings jacket and had his hands in the pockets. No hat. There were ten other people scattered on the platform, waiting. Ellis stood at the exact spot where he knew the car would stop and the door would open so he could rush in and get his seat. Sydney walked with some others and stood near him.

The sound of the oncoming train was getting a bit louder. On the other end of the platform someone yelled. Sydney looked and so did everyone else. A man was screaming at a woman holding a child. Most of the words weren't audible but it was clearly a family fight. Sydney edged forward until Ellis stood right in front of her. His toes were only inches from the edge of the platform and he was looking toward the argument.

She hadn't planned it, but there it was. Sydney pushed him hard with both hands in the small of his back. He called out, a shriek, not words like "help me".

He landed on the tracks, cracking his head. It was a loud popping sound, almost like hitting a drum. His hands were still in his pockets. Then everything happened at once.

People began yelling, saying "Stop the train, get that man off the tracks, did you see that man fall?" A tall fellow in

Army fatigues nearly jumped down to help but didn't have time.

The train came in seconds later, screeching brakes as the operator saw the body but was too late to stop. There was no bump like an automobile would make if it ran over a rabbit or a person. The doors opened just when and where they should. Everyone rushed out, no one rushed in, but the train was going nowhere. The transit police were on the scene right away.

Sydney stood and waited to be arrested. It didn't matter. Ellis was dead and she did it and was glad. And proud. Patrick and her mother were avenged.

But nothing happened. No one approached her. Apparently she hadn't been seen pushing him. So she just went home and sat for days waiting for them to come for her. There had been cameras, and they showed the video on television over and over. But she appeared as just a small dark figure. No identifiable face shot. She had gotten away with it.

Now she was free. But practical matters remained. The money and credit were gone, she was almost out of food and she needed a job. She had no skills but knew some things. Things she had studied and thought she would be good at.

Sydney went to the Parthenon where she knew there was a job opening.

Over the next year she worked out the plan to start her own business helping others solve situations similar to her own. She named it HumanPestControl.com.

PART ONE
Ten Year's Later

1

Three contracts to kill Earl the Cannibal arrived within forty-eight hours after he was exonerated by a jury and put back on the street. The calls for the hit came from three sources via encrypted emails to Sydney's website.

Earl's crimes had been truly horrific. The media said he kidnapped women and children, kept them awhile in a soundproof room in his basement where no one knew, even after the fact, exactly what happened to them. The rumors were that he killed and ate them, though he denied it. Still, the name Earl the Cannibal stuck. He wouldn't talk to the police when he was finally arrested and didn't confess at first. There were only sections and pieces of the victims in his garage freezer so it was useless speculation as to whether they were first tortured or sexually assaulted. The bones they dug up were jumbled together, making a puzzling job for the pathologist.

But there was no question that he was a very, very bad man. He was considered so evil that the citizens and police in the small town near Zephyr Hills, Florida where he lived took extra steps to be sure he was convicted. Those extra steps led to his release.

Sydney's potential internet clients were cagey, not wanting to reveal who they were until they felt comfortable that their identities would be kept confidential. Sydney felt the same way. It wouldn't do to be set up by the cops in a sting operation. Security was as airtight as she could make it and Sydney didn't think the authorities had any way of tracing her through her offshore website. But you never knew. That was why she checked out the clients nearly as much as the potential victim they wanted eliminated. Her research revealed that two of the new inquiries were from family members of one of Earl's victims. A natural and normal reaction, she had found. Kill the bad guy that took one of their own. She knew just how they felt.

The third request was from a man unrelated to any of the cannibal's victims who claimed to be incensed at the miscarriage of justice. That sort of email was not unusual in these kinds of cases, but when pressed the outraged weren't usually serious enough to pay for the services they requested. And it wasn't necessarily the killing of someone a client wanted when they went to her site. What they actually wanted, what would satisfy them, was an unspecified revenge—to have the situation somehow made right. That was Sydney's specialty.

When Sydney finally took on an assignment she would assure the client that they would be satisfied but the method she used to carry it out was entirely up to her and would not be shared until after the fact—if then. More often than not she could solve a problem non-lethally by, for example, creating an unexplained fire or explosion which might destroy a home or business. Or perhaps set up a situation that would create a legal or business crisis for the victim. But Earl was definitely on the hook for a permanent pest control solution. He fit the criteria of justice that had not been served and there was no satisfactory option for someone like him other than his complete elimination.

During a six-week trial, his attorneys found that potentially exculpatory evidence had never been revealed to the defense as was legally required, and other evidence had been destroyed by one of the police officers. The court ruled that there had been no probable cause to search his property without a warrant and that therefore the search of his property was illegal. Since the search was illegal any evidence discovered in the search was inadmissible. Fruit of the poisonous tree, they called it. Made for a tough case to prosecute.

Two of the alleged witnesses to an alleged abduction of one of the children recanted on the witness stand, one in tears, saying that they had just wanted to make Earl pay. That didn't look so good to the jury. Personal items of the children had even been planted inside Earl's house by the police in an attempt to make the case appear more solid. The court said that given police and prosecutorial misconduct, most of the evidence they had could not be heard by the jury.

The jury had been sequestered so they didn't hear most of the damning facts that were so widely reported on television and in the news. The public was convinced that he had committed the crimes but the jury had been denied the information that would have led to his conviction and eventual execution. Double jeopardy meant that constitutionally he couldn't be charged again or retried for the murders. There was talk of a federal prosecution but nothing came of it.

So he was free. Television commentators speculated as to whether he would go back to his old ways, but the authorities were powerless to control him or confine him. People were outraged when a month after the trial and his acquittal Earl was interviewed by a weekly tabloid newspaper. Rumors were that he was paid for the interview. He didn't deny doing the crimes and even provided details of how he might have picked one person over another based on his particular sick preferences. Hypothetically, of course. The public at large, and the affected families in particular, were beyond angry. Now he was living somewhere in Florida, but his exact location wasn't publically released.

Sydney tried to be dispassionate and very selective about her assignments. Only a few requests for help fit her criteria. Her requirements had nothing to do with her personal feelings. The real question was whether all other avenues had been dead ends and whether she could provide a satisfactory solution. This one fit the bill, but could they pay the bill? Nothing was free and she couldn't justify the huge risks she must take unless it was worth her while. And she had to remain anonymous. Gunning Earl down at home or in the street might be popular, and she had done it on more than one occasion but it was risky and not her style. Contrived accidents were her preference.

Too much time at the computer, she thought. Sydney pushed away from her desk, grabbed a soda from her mini-refrigerator, thought a second, changed it to two beers and went looking for Oscar. She would discuss the situation with him, but knew he wouldn't want her to take the case—or any case that might expose her to harm. She found him in the gallery at the front of the building taking down the current show and packing the paintings that hadn't sold. The building was railroad style, long and narrow with the gallery in the storefront, then Oscar's law office, behind that his studio, then her secure steel-doored office and at the rear, a small storeroom and bathrooms. They lived upstairs in a building-length open-loft apartment.

"You can do that tomorrow, you know," Sydney said, opening and handing him a bottle.

"Everything can be put off until tomorrow, but I have time now. Unless you have something more exciting in mind." He clinked bottles with her and dropped his screwdriver on a packing case.

"I like your new look," she said, eyeing him up and

down. He was nearly a foot taller than her and typically wore dress pants and a golf shirt. "Jeans, worn-out tennies, ripped T-shirt. Kind of a day-laborer thing. It works better than attorney for me. You should get a tattoo."

"They're all uniforms. Wear what works for the situation, I say. Besides, look at you. Your tiny self all in black even when it's a hundred degrees in full Florida August sunshine. You look like either a small ninja or a New Yorker."

She gave him a full grin, standing close and looking up at him. "I wear this stuff just because I know it turns you on. Let's go upstairs. I want to talk to you about a possible case."

Oscar always let her go first up the stairs to the apartment and she knew it wasn't because he was being polite. They went to the front of the apartment, then out to the New Orleans style balcony overlooking the quiet street. There was an ocean breeze coming off the Palm Beaches across Lake Worth and the building faced north, shading the balcony and mitigating the ninety-plus heat. This was their spot to end the day, sitting in deck chairs with their feet on the wrought-iron railing. They sat for a while in comfortable silence, finishing their beers.

"So about the new case," Sydney began. "It's a very bad man. The worst, in fact. I bet you could name him in three guesses."

"Earl the cannibal?"

"Bingo. Okay. One guess."

"You sure you need to go after him? There must be a list a mile long of willing assassins."

"Yeah, well it's not going to be easy if I decide to do it. And mostly people talk and bitch about things but do nothing, so the list isn't that long. The police are going to protect him no matter how they feel about it so I always have to work around them."

"You're a pretty good shot. You could do the sniper thing. You wouldn't have to get up close and personal to the guy that way."

"Guns are a last resort. I don't want to be on the run while trying to ditch a weapon with all that entails. And it's noisy and silencers throw off the accuracy. So I have to give it a lot of thought. I also don't know if they can afford me."

"It's been a while since you took an extreme case like this. Do you need the money?" Oscar tipped up his bottle to get the last drop.

"It's a matter of principle. I'm not Wonder Woman trying to solve the world's problems. What I do, I do well, and I expect to be paid for it. That's the way it is. One day I'll retire and I want to do so with some kind of style. I was hoping you'd like to be involved in that aspect of my career." They leaned toward each other and bumped fists.

"I can go on the job with you as soon as I get this show packed and shipped." Oscar said. He was sincere and would help willingly, Sydney knew, but she worked alone as much as she could. The main reason to keep Oscar out of it was to protect him. He was an attorney and she didn't want him directly involved in her business. He had a lot to lose if caught. His help was typically advice, information gathering, and sometimes acting as a lookout or driver. This wasn't his deal and he would get involved only to try to help and do his best to cover her back. It was a mutual love thing he did on his end because he worried about her.

"If I take the case I can do it on my own. You don't need the risk or exposure. It should be safe. A staged accident is what I'm thinking, but I have to know more before I make a plan."

Before they went to bed she sent encrypted emails

through an untraceable proxy node to the three would-be clients. No one could track her IP address that way to locate her computer. She asked for further information, specifically if they knew where Earl was hiding out after his release. She would determine the fee to be charged after seeing how much work would be involved. Sometimes it was easier than she initially thought. But there was no question that Earl needed to be erased.

2

A day later Sydney had heard from all three potential clients. One backed out with an apology, saying she would be no better a person than Earl if she had him killed. The other woman was an aunt of a victim, had no information on him other than what was in the papers and on television, but still wanted to go ahead if she could afford it. The male client was a better prospect. He said he knew how to find Earl and asked how much would it cost and what was the procedure?

Sydney needed only one client. She thought it unethical to take money from two people for the same job. So the family member got her condolences and she sent an email to the remaining client asking for his name, telephone number, and Earl's location. There would be no in-person meeting for security on both their parts, she explained.

After confirming Earl's whereabouts she would develop a plan. Then the client would be given instructions on where to wire half the fee. It would be sent to an offshore bank in a country not friendly to the United States—Venezuela in this case. The best solution for payment she had found so far. She had started out her business requiring that cash be sent to a mail drop that in turn forwarded the package to another drop. But that had proved unreliable and she had nearly been caught doing the pickup. She then considered using Bitcoins or some other online currency, but was unsure about their security, even though drug dealers made occasional use of them and their value was uncertain.

The current system was configured so that the wire transfer money was only in the target bank for a matter of minutes before ninety-five percent of it was automatically transferred to another offshore account in the name of one of her private companies. Five percent was the bank's commission. Oscar was intentionally unaware of her system's structure, wanting plausible deniability, though he accepted what she did for a living.

A half hour later the man emailed back. He would give only his first name, Luke, and a telephone number that she assumed would be from a disposable cell. That's what she would have done. But had he had enough time to arrange that? Probably not, so he would be using his own telephone. As to location, the client said Earl was living in Tampa in a run-down section near Ybor City, renting a room under an assumed name. The police had helped relocate him for his own protection, and, Sydney suspected, to get him out of their jurisdiction. He was being given no police protection.

Even though he was an admitted sex offender and killer he wasn't in the public registry available online because he hadn't been officially convicted. The registry would have given his address. His job was as a night janitor at a Cuban grocery in Ybor. She assumed they set that up so he would have no contact with other people while working alone on the night shift. But the job was supposedly temporary and Earl would likely be moving on soon according to the client. Time was of the essence. She had five days. So the job, if she took it, sounded doable and not as difficult as it might have been.

Tampa was about two hundred miles from West Palm where Sydney and Oscar lived so the job would require several days out of town. Factoring in the risk involved, the high profile nature of the victim, and the desirable result of erasing Earl, she quoted a fee of one hundred thousand dollars.

She traced the telephone number Luke supplied to see who owned it. It was a church. The Gracious Lord Temple in Orlando. She looked them up. An independent Pentecostal-type organization. So the potential client was either an employee or the head pastor. She needed to find out how serious the guy really was and if he was legitimate. He could merely be the lead man in a sting, cooperating with the cops, or he could be a legitimate client. Either way she needed to know more. The website revealed that Pastor Luke Anger was the head man at the church. There was only a small group picture revealing he was an older white man with blond hair. So the pastor was more than likely the client; how many Lukes could there be?

Sydney called the number.

In the old days Sydney used an analog voice-scrambler to disguise her voice when making a call to a blind number. That technology was good for the time, but with the right equipment the FBI or a big police department could unscramble it and pull a voice print that could be used to identify her. With the coming of the digital age she had upgraded to a text-to-speech software program downloaded to her smart-phone. She could carry on a conversation in twenty-five languages using dozens of accents with either a male or female voice.

She could do Donald Duck or Darth Vader as well. She also had voice recognition software that would go voice to text if she wanted to talk to someone in a language she did not know. What would they come up with next? The voice she chose to call Luke with sounded like an Australian male. Her app allowed her to text what she wanted to say and the chosen voice spoke the words she typed in. That meant a short delay in responding to the person on the other end, but had not been a problem so far.

A man answered. "Pastor Luke here."

"Pastor Luke? I am calling on behalf of the pest control

service you hired."

He had answered on the first ring. "You can't call me here. Calls can be traced. Use email if you need to reach me. I have a private account I'll give you." Luke spoke quickly but in a loud whisper.

"Ha," Sydney's disguised voice said. "You think email's private? I have a secure telephone line so no one will trace me. Can't say the same for you, though. I can reach you when I need to, don't worry."

"What is it you want? I'll send whatever money you need, but discretion is paramount."

"I want to know why you are willing to pay to have the cannibal killed. Did he harm a friend or relative? Maybe a church member?"

"No. Nothing like that. Listen, I am a man of God, but still a man with all of man's frailties. What this cannibal has done sickens me and I cannot in good conscience see Earl Santiago walk God's earth as if nothing he did was wrong. I'm not waiting for him to get his punishment in hell or get a chance to kill another innocent child. I want his hell to start now. A person like that won't stop. I would smite him myself if I thought I could."

Smite him. Sydney loved that. She smiled. "So you want me to kill him because he's a killer. Very Christian of you. Upholds a long tradition."

"Don't talk smart to me. This is right. But nothing you do can link Santiago's death to the church or to me. I have to do this. I feel a moral obligation to the community to avenge the deaths of the children. I love the children."

"If I take the job," Sydney said, "you can be sure that you will have anonymity—so long as the second half payment is made on completion. You will have nothing to worry about. We both want discretion. I'll text you the bank routing number for the first half of the fee. That's fifty thousand you should be sending along in the next twelve hours. I hope you can afford it because receiving the second half when the job's done is very important to me." She disconnected, texted the numbers, then tapped the cell on her hip, thinking. Then dropped the phone to the ground, stomped it twice, and scattered the pieces in separate street-side trash cans.

3

Ybor City is no longer a city. Now a part of Tampa it was originally settled in the late nineteenth century as a cigar making center by Vincente Martinez Ybor who moved his cigar factory first from Cuba to Key West, and then to the east side of Tampa. For fifty years it was a flourishing community of Spanish, Cubans, and Italians all working in the cigar trade, producing at its peak five hundred million cigars annually. In 1929 the great depression killed the cigar business as smokers switched to the cheaper cigarettes and Ybor City itself died. Its buildings deteriorated, most everyone moved away. Later, to accommodate the need for more highways to move around the burgeoning Florida population, a great swath of the area was bulldozed to allow construction of Intrastate 4.

Then, as often happens in blighted areas, artists discovered the cheap living, studio, and gallery space and revitalization began, eventually out-pricing and displacing most of the artists with clubs, restaurants, cigar bars, and trendy shops. Sydney wondered where the artists were doing their urban renewal work now. A couple of entrepreneurs had even started making cigars again in Ybor on a boutique basis.

Sydney had stopped there several years before as a tourist, going one evening for dinner after spending the day on St. Petersburg Beach. But this was an assignment. So no leisurely dinner and drinks. And precious little sleep for the next couple of days.

She took State Road 60 West which ended in Tampa and avoided the Turnpike. There would be no paper trail, no EZ-Pass record. To do surveillance she rented a nondescript Ford Taurus with black-out windows from a local agency in

West Palm. It would have been hard to do a proper stakeout on her Harley and the Mustang was too flashy. A vehicle with a roadmap GPS and screen built into the dashboard had been offered but she didn't want that. She would have had to disable it so her movements couldn't be tracked and didn't need the hassle. As it was, she still had to knock out the Lojack GPS anti-theft system and that was trouble enough.

The road cut east to west across the state, running through a half dozen small towns on the way. The first fifty miles or so was vast expanses of swamp and grazing land that gave way to citrus and industry. A truckload of oranges blocked her way and slowed her down in one of the few areas where it was still a two-lane. As she approached Tampa the road widened and filled on both sides with retail, offices, and fast-food restaurants. Not as busy as West Palm, but not far from it. And this was summer, not "The Season" when all the snowbirds would balloon the population.

Earl's rooming house was on a side street bordering an industrial area. She watched it from a block away all the first day. His picture had been all over the news during his trial so she was sure she would recognize him. He didn't come out during the day, but several others did. The roommates came back in late afternoon, probably returning from work. Two had cars, which they parked at the curb, and there was a bicycle chained to a pole next to the porch. The only delivery was by a mail carrier.

At least five people shared the house, all men. If the young raggedy guy she was watching hadn't been sitting on his own porch smoking and drinking a beer, his appearance would have pegged him as homeless. A scruffy bunch.

It looked like someone had cut the place up into a rooming house. Its bones indicated it was likely a nice place sixty years ago. Probably had housed generations of moms, dads, and kids. The house was a wood-frame two-story with a covered porch on which sagged two worn sofas. Beer cans sat at attention on the spoked railing. The screen in the front door was missing and a squat spotted dog wandered in and out. The green roof on Earl's house had been patched with black shingles. The block he lived on had only three houses on the left side of the street, but the empty lots between showed they had once had neighbors.

Maybe the missing houses were victims of a fire, or perhaps they rotted and were torn down. No vegetation survived except some overgrown Brazilian Pepper trees in a tangled mass on the back edge of the lots. The houses were only a few feet from the broken sidewalk and pavement. An alley ran behind the houses, but there were no garages. Dust, dirt, sun, and sand.

So the idea of taking him down at home in his sleep seemed a bad one. Unworkable. Too uncertain when people would be coming by. And Sydney didn't like to hurt a dog. She had had an unfortunate encounter with one in the past. The animal hadn't fared well. She liked to blame its upbringing rather than the dog itself. Poor nurture, not bad nature.

She needed to see the set-up at Earl's workplace and moved the car to watch the Cuban grocery from a distance during his shift.

This was more promising. Earl's job presented multiple opportunities to take him out. He worked from ten in the evening until four in the morning mopping and cleaning the Havana Market a few blocks from his room and rode the bicycle there and back. She considered clipping him with the car but wanted certainty. Broken bones wouldn't complete the contract. No one stayed with him at the store when he worked, but he locked himself in except when he brought trash out to the dumpster in back. That was one opportunity. She wanted to check one more night, but thought the store would be where he would meet his well-deserved fatal accident. There would be no deliveries and no customers at night; so no interruptions or bothersome witnesses to be concerned about.

Sydney had rented a motel room about ten miles away on the edge of the city the day she arrived. The Flamingo Motor Lodge was concrete-block painted a pale Caribbean-pink with peeling lime-green shutters. It looked to have been built in the late fifties or early sixties. The motel office housing the manager was near the street and the rooms were single story, all in a row, each with a plastic chair and outside light next to the door. No pool. No grass. No other customers. It still had the original neon sign in the office window: "We're air-conditioned". It was frowzy, cheap, fairly clean and would do. Plus they took cash, which was an advantage for someone not wanting to leave a trail.

She drove around the area scoping out primary escape routes if needed and places to buy supplies, then stopped at the Havana Market and went in for a little reconnaissance. She wore a shoulder-length blond wig under a floppy straw hat, red beach cover-up dress, sunglasses, and sandals. Tourist attire.

Sydney was trying on ten-dollar sunglasses from a rotating display near the front door as she looked around, spotting the security cameras. Bars barricaded the display windows.

Cameras were trained on the door, the cash register, and the customer counter. Later she noticed another one outside aimed at the rear door. The aisles were crowded with large bags of rice, beans, flour, and cornmeal. There was a section with cleaning and kitchen supplies and the usual assortment of canned goods and paper products. Nearly all the signs and some of the labels on the food were in Spanish. The vegetable section was sorry looking with wilted greens and aging tropical vegetables and fruit.

Sydney examined a prickly pear cactus pad, wondering how it should be prepared. She peeked into the back room. There was a restroom sign in Spanish on a door in the hallway. It appeared to be unisex.

She opened the door to the restroom tentatively, flipped on the light, and looked in. It was reasonably clean and had no strong odor. She went in and locked the door. A ceiling vent fan came on when the light switch was flipped. Using her Swiss Army Knife she took the cover plate off the light switch, identified the power line to the fan, disconnected it and clipped it off so short that it would be a complicated job to replace. The fan stopped. Then she replaced the cover and proceeded to the checkout to pay for a bottle of water. There were only two people working the store that she could see and there were no other customers.

Earl came out of the house in the early evening, walking toward Seventh Street, the main drag in Ybor that had been closed off to accommodate the throngs of tourists that frequented all the night clubs, galleries, and restaurants. This was not a fancy pedestrian mall. The street they wandered on was still asphalt with crumbling pavement, manhole covers, crushed cigarette butts, black chewing gum spots, and spilled beer.

He stopped and leaned against a tree watching a group of pre-teens playing soccer. There were lots of moms and dads around, so Sydney wasn't worried he was going to try and pick off one of the kids. Right now. And soon never. A police cruiser drove slowly by and Sydney thought that she and Earl shared a common desire to not be interviewed by them.

It was like a festival downtown. Sydney followed Earl

by walking on the side of the street, ducking through the crowds but staying close. Earl cooperated by walking down the middle among the crowds standing, talking, drinking, smoking, and dancing. Some of the storefront windows were like stages with dancers and other performers working behind the display windows. An artist was making large abstract paintings in one window, flinging paint and dancing as he created. Loud live Latin music emanated from multiple venues.

The night was hot and humid and the women in the throngs had dressed for it, much skin showing. Young gang-banger types with loose pants—their own uniform, stood around joking and talking and there was a heavy police presence all patrolling in pairs.

She almost lost him when he ducked into a doorway but found Earl drinking beer at an upstairs jazz club, but he had no food. Sydney sat at the small bar, watching him in the mirror, drinking a plain tonic on ice. The room was poorly lit but Earl looked as normal as anyone else, not as the monster he actually was. He eventually made his way back home after getting some grilled meat on a stick from a street vendor. Later he made his regular bike ride to work.

Nothing significant happened that night. There were no deliveries and he had no visitors. Earl started by emptying the wastebaskets and taking out all the cardboard boxes from which inventory had been emptied to the dumpster behind the building. That meant the back door would be open briefly. She could have killed him right then, but much preferred to arrange an apparent accidental death since fewer questions would be asked by the authorities. There was no reason to be on the run as a fugitive if there was an alternative.

Besides, she had an idea that would make his death look like the result of his own stupidity, which she felt suited the situation. It would also not be pleasant for him. A plus, given her personal need to make him pay for the pain he had caused so many. She checked the dumpster by skirting around the back of the lot, away from the security camera. It was nearly empty so it was safe to assume another garbage pickup wouldn't be made for several days.

Sydney's experience had been that the cops didn't bother to investigate too deeply if she supplied a plausible cause of death to hang their hats on. They would probably be as pleased as everyone else that Earl was dead, whatever the cause. She couldn't see what he did inside the store except when he mopped the floors near the front window. He stayed there until four in the morning, and then rode home. She watched his house for a few hours but there was no activity other than a light going on in what must be his bedroom, then off. In the morning she headed back to the Flamingo, stopping for some coffee and take-out breakfast, then hit the bed.

About four hours later she went back to the house. Earl's bike was still home. She had to assume he was still sleeping so she went shopping at a local Walmart. The plan she devised could be carried out with equipment and materials available at any hardware. She selected a B-B gun, the best chemical mask they had, one used by painters to avoid inhaling fumes, bought a quart of muriatic acid and some swimmer's goggles. She didn't think any other weapons were needed, but she had a backup hammerless snub-nosed .357 in a holster at the small of her back, and if necessary her martial arts skills could be employed. Her hand-to-hand combat skills were good but she didn't like to rely on them because of her size. Being only five-two and thin, a big guy who got lucky enough to get his hands on her could be difficult to handle. Of course Earl wasn't a big guy.

She repeated the Earl-watch for another night. This

time Sydney waited until Earl went home, then snuck around the back of the dumpster next door to the market, took careful aim with the air gun, and fired at the security light at the back of the building. The shot went high and to the right, so she adjusted and shot again, taking out the light from about fifty yards on the second shot. It wasn't the light that worried her; it was the security camera over the back door.

She couldn't easily get within shooting range of the small camera lens without being photographed if the light was on, but could if it were off. One shot took out the lens when she approached it. The BB gun wasn't very powerful and didn't do much more than pop a hole in the glass of the light and camera. But it took them out efficiently without the sound of crashing glass or the report from a firearm.

Back at the motel she showered and stayed awake, thinking about what was to come until the draperies filtered the morning light into the room. After a few hours' sleep she checked and rechecked her equipment for the night's mission.

There was an empty lot near the store that didn't have security cameras so was ideal for parking. When Earl arrived and was inside, Sydney went to the back of the store dressed all in black and wearing a silk ski mask that held her hair tight to her head.

On schedule Earl carried a load of cardboard and garbage bags to the dumpster. The back door opened outward spilling light into the parking lot. Sydney had hidden at the hinge side of the door and slipped inside as Earl walked to the dumpster with his arms full.

He returned to the store, whistling as if he was at peace. Maybe he was. They say sociopaths have no conscience. Then again, Sydney didn't feel bad about what she was about to do, so what did that make her? Justified? Or was she not so different from him? Should she repent again? Seeing him close up, she could see that Earl was a little skinny guy with a pale complexion. It didn't look like he spent any time outside. In Florida most people had some sort of tan. Not Earl. He was pasty-white with a teenager's acne, though she knew he was thirty-one. He looked ordinary. Not like a child-killer and cannibal. Maybe a clerk, or a janitor in this case. It would be no contest in a one-on-one with him. But that was only part of the plan. She waited while he started his next chore: mopping the floors.

She stayed out of sight in the store room while he prepared to fill the mop bucket with water from the bathroom slop sink. It was a galvanized five-gallon pail on wheels with a ringer that operated by a plunger type handle when the wet mop was inserted in the top. He was still whistling when she came up behind him, spun him around, pinned him to the wall with her forearm across his skinny neck and crushed his testicles with her knee.

"You knew you were going to have to pay for your sins one day, didn't you Earl?" She shoved him into the toilet room, rammed the door shut and secured it with the mop handle jammed against the door next to the knob and pressed against the opposite wall of the narrow hall.

While he banged and pushed on the door and screamed for help she shut off the main power at the electrical panel and found her way to the store shelves and took three bottles of toilet bowl cleaner and two gallons of household bleach back to the bathroom hallway and flipped the lights back on. It would look odd for the interior lights to be off to any passerby and she needed no extra attention right now. The gas mask was the first item from her bag of supplies. Then she put on the goggles to protect her eyes and donned heavy rubber gloves. The interior cameras, had they been on, would have shown her almost as a B-movie outer space alien what with the black body suit, gloves, gas mask, and goggles. Earl was yelling and banging on the door but he was going nowhere and she ignored him.

The toilet bowl cleaner was the first thing to go into the mop bucket. On top of that she added the half-gallon of muriatic acid. The toilet cleaner contained sulphuric acid so the two acids would be powerful enough to activate the third ingredient—the bleach.

Sydney pulled back the mask and deep breathed to hyper-oxygenate, then held her breath and replaced the mask. She had been practicing and could keep from breathing for nearly two minutes—not completely trusting the mask. It would be enough time. She quickly poured the gallons of bleach into the bucket, trying not to splash. The mixture fizzed, and began to almost steam, the poisonous gas rising out. She opened the door to the toilet and shoved Earl back inside when he tried to rush her, his head thudding against the rear wall.

She pushed the steaming bucket in and re-secured the door. As bad as Earl was, she didn't want to hear what came next and stepped outside and leaned against the wall while the chemicals did their work. She was an executioner, not a sadist. This would be an appropriate time for a cigarette if she smoked. Or a cigar in honor of Ybor.

When mixed with the acids, the bleach released all its chlorine as a lethal gas in the enclosed space of the toilet. There was no longer an exhaust fan to dilute the toxic air. Chlorine gas was the very same that the Germans first used as a poison gas in World War One in the trenches. The gas caused extremely painful burning and permanent damage to the eyes, throat, and lungs. Earl's throat would swell and his lungs would fill with fluid. Of those in the war who somehow survived after being exposed to a diluted gas in the open air, many would be blinded or seriously injured. Earl however would die painfully and fairly quickly in the concentrated environment of the small room. Dying painfully in a toilet. Now that was justice.

This sort of accident actually happened occasionally. Sydney had read about it in her research. Wanting to clean everything thoroughly, an especially eager but inexperienced cleaner might mix together ingredients that shouldn't be mixed together. Who reads the warnings on the labels anyway?

She stood outside in the dark waiting. The only light was that from the open doorway sliding out conically into the parking lot toward the dumpster. She could hear the faint screams from inside, but tried to think of other things. An oddity lay on the ground next to the dumpster itself. A wilted rose in a small glass vase. Maybe something thrown out and salvaged that some dumpster diver was planning on picking up later. And a small black book next to it. A strange world we humans inhabit, she thought.

After the noises from the toilet room subsided, Sydney waited another ten minutes, then propped the back door to keep it open, unblocked and opened the toilet door, and stepped back outside to let the fumes dissipate. She flipped on the power and made a final check a few minutes later. Earl was clearly dead. He lay on the floor, his eyes open and bloodshot, his tongue pushed past his teeth. He had vomited blood that was fizzing in the acid on the floor. His face and hands were blistered. He had dumped the caustic mixture from the mop pail, but that had only made it spread into the air faster. His jeans had bleached white where they soaked up the liquid.

Sydney took the bottles of toilet cleaner and bleach and pressed Earl's fingers around them to create prints, then set the bottles carefully in a row outside the door. She left by the back exit, which she left propped open. No point in poisoning the innocents on the first shift when they came in, she thought. She took her bag and dropped in the gas mask, goggles and the muriatic acid bottle, then dropped the bag and the air gun in a dumpster several miles down the road. Being extra careful, she would burn her clothing and rubber gloves. No trace evidence that way, and she had heard that someone had once been convicted when the cops turned a pair of rubber gloves inside out and took finger prints from them.

She did not return to the Flamingo.

4

Sydney had never had a hobby other than polishing and acquiring skills that would help her in her off-the-books business. She had mastered most small arms, was an expert with bow and arrow, mastered lock-picking, could make explosive devices of many kinds, was skilled in several of the martial arts—even including boxing, had taken a police driving course, had a captain's license for offshore boating, and had excelled in her fencing lessons. She had excellent mechanical aptitude and was considering getting a pilot's license.

But she had no non-work-related hobbies.

So it was a revelation to her that she would take up and enjoy the art of bonsai. She stumbled into it, literally, while helping Oscar man his booth at Artfest-By-The-Sea, the annual art fair in Jupiter, Florida.

It was Oscar's first try at selling his artwork out-of-doors, though he knew a number of art fair artists who had spent their lives doing it. He had always sold his small figurative sculpture in his own space, the Rose Madder Gallery in West Palm Beach. Rose Madder was actually a color, but non-art folks assumed it was the gallery owner's name and often asked if Ms. Madder was in when visiting. An artist friend had convinced him to apply for the fair, explaining that he would benefit not just from additional sales, but would meet lots of prospective customers and other artists. Networking, she said, was the key to success. Oscar wasn't much of a networker but had always wanted to try the art fair thing.

During the three months leading up to the fair he had produced a dozen new ceramic sculptures to add to his existing inventory. He was able to borrow a ten-by-ten canopy for the space he would occupy in case of rain and planned to use sculpture pedestals from the gallery for his display. On the day before the show opened he and Sydney set up the shelving and canopy and placed the sculpture, then zipped the place up ready to open in the morning. The sponsor provided security and assured them the artwork would be safe.

It rained steadily the first day and they huddled under the canopy but the crowds still came. The fair was held on a stretch of A-1-A bordering the Atlantic near the Jupiter Inlet. Each participant was assigned a space along either side of the roadway. There was a food court area bounded by trailers and tents selling fair food: hot dogs, kettle corn, ice cream, sodas, various fried meat sandwiches, and even a beer tent. Then he sat for two days in his canvas director's chair, talking to those of the several hundred visitors who stepped into his booth. He handed out postcards, looked at the other exhibitors while Sydney watched the merchandise, and near the end of day two both of them were thoroughly bored.

Most of the booths had artwork by local painters and potters, one of which was where Sydney ran into the bonsai guy. He was selling hand-made ceramic pottery, primarily for use as bonsai pots. These were low-sided dishes glazed in different colors and in all different sizes. Part of his display showed how they were used with a collection of his own miniature bonsai trees planted in his pots.

Sydney had had enough of sitting in the booth by the end of day one, but tried to keep a team face. On day two she was walking through the crowd watching a pair of uniformed sheriff's deputies who seemed to be looking for someone—whom she hoped wasn't her—when she tripped over a highway reflector in the pavement and fell into the booth of the bonsai man. She rolled and her foot hit the edge of a shelf, propelling one of the display bonsai into the air, then she slid on her back and caught the one she knocked over, holding it above her, undamaged. The crowd applauded and the guy was surprised, but was relieved nothing had been destroyed. To make up for the accident she bought the bonsai, which was a small ficus in a green glazed ceramic pot. It came with a tiny ceramic Chinese man who sat under the miniature tree.

She asked questions to find out how to care for it and bought a paperback from the seller on bonsai history, as well as care and maintenance.

Oscar was astounded and teased her since she had never displayed any interest in plants or gardening. She had always seemed barely aware of nature. A New York concrete and stone kind of person. It was contrary to his perception of her character. She seemed not to be a hands-in-the-dirt kind.

"It's not like gardening," she explained, back at his booth. "It's more like having a child or getting a dog. I'm now responsible for a living thing that might well outlive me. If I don't care for it properly it will die. If I apply myself, learn about the process and treat it right, the plant will grow more beautiful as years go by and will be admired by all."

Oscar sold nothing during the show, but had kept track and told Sydney that in two days he had received one hundred nineteen complements similar to "I love your work".

"One art fair is enough for me," Oscar said. Sydney agreed and they packed up and went home.

She built a shelf for the new bonsai on the upper balcony where it would get the morning sun and went to a local bonsai shop and spent several hundred dollars on books, special soil, tools, and other supplies.

"This is just the beginning, you know," Oscar warned. "Pretty soon you'll get another, then another. I'll probably have to put on a third story to house them all."

"I'm sure you will do whatever it takes to keep me

happy." Sydney was examining the tree, trying to determine where and if to snip a limb or whether she should coil some soft copper wire around a branch to make it turn. She referred to her books, but was reluctant to trim anything. Once trimmed it couldn't be untrimmed.

"Did you name it?"

"You don't name plants. And don't make fun. I like doing this. You have your sculpture and I can have this."

"No argument here. I like it that you like it."

"There are bonsai that have been handed down like heirlooms generation to generation. There's one that they say is eight-hundred years old. They're gifts to be left to those who follow."

"So this looks like a lifetime commitment. You should have children so you can leave Freddy to them."

"Don't name my tree. And does that mean you want children?"

"Just saying." He retreated quickly to his office downstairs, stopping first to feed Jesse, his elderly blond Labrador Retriever.

Oscar was tied to the gallery for the next week, completing a proposal for a public sculpture commission and accepting shipped and hand-delivered paintings for a new show. About half had arrived and were out of their cases and temporarily leaning against the gallery walls until everything was there in order to determine the best arrangement for hanging.

The art responsibilities left little room for his law practice. It had turned into a part-time occupation and he discouraged rather than encouraged new clients; though it seemed there was always someone calling him back to the profession. He seriously considered not renewing his license but was reluctant to burn that boat in case he needed to sail it again. At the moment he had only two clients. Oscar hadn't yet reached forty but was semi-retired from the law, preferring creating and selling sculpture to solving other people's problems. The occasional legal client was what paid most of the bills. He didn't ask for Sydney's help and she finally gave up offering to shoulder some of the finances. His attitude was a macho guy thing, she said to him. She didn't add that it also seemed sexist to her. And she had a lot of cash, more than him, so that was not the issue.

The bonsai needed no more work, so Sydney went to her own secure office downstairs to check for new possible Pest Control clients. They came to her through her special encrypted email account that had been routed through so many servers that it was untraceable even if a suspicious person had the resources and knowledge to try to track her internet activity. So far she had stayed out of serious trouble by being very careful as to what cases she took and by doing deep research on the victims she chose and the methods to be used on them.

Thorough research equaled good security. She also investigated the request to be sure the victim deserved punishment and that she wasn't abetting some personal vendetta. The website, HumanPestControl.com, was her sole source for business. If possible she tried to take cases within driving distance. Travel created more opportunities for the authorities to track her movements through airlines, hotels, and rental cars. There was less of a paper trail by staying close to home.

She sorted through several calls for help. A lot were for things like collecting back child support or getting even with a cheating spouse. She wasn't a collection agency and didn't take most domestic cases. She also did not get involved in commercial disputes. That's why we all pay judges and lawyers, she told Oscar. She was not a private investigator so would not look for missing persons; at least so far. Her experience had been that if someone was missing it was either because they wanted to be or because they were dead. Her niche was providing justice where the legal system could not or would not act. That was more than a full-time job.

5

Until Sydney revealed her secret occupation to Oscar, which was after she was confident it wouldn't change his opinion of her, Sydney had been a loner. Oscar didn't ask a lot of questions even now, didn't know everything about her past, and said he didn't want to. She considered telling all, but keeping secrets was ingrained and hard to change. She would share with him moving forward, but he was right as to there being no benefit revisiting her sometimes violent history. Having someone who loved you and being able to be completely honest with him was a gift she cherished. But all good things come with a price.

She and Oscar were on the upper balcony that evening, watching the traffic on the two-lane street and the occasional pedestrian. They were above the street lights and so invisible to walkers below.

"Sydney?"

"Yes, Oscar?" She was watching a man trying to walk three leashed Jack Russell terriers that couldn't agree on which direction to go.

"Sydney, have you ever heard of the concept of marital privilege?"

She looked over at him in the dim light, grinning. "You mean where the man can have his way with his woman, no matter what she says?"

"No. That's a whole other subject. It's a legal term. It means that in a court of law a wife cannot be compelled to testify against her husband and vice-versa. It's a legal privilege, like the one for doctor-patient, priest-penitent or attorney-client."

"Gotcha."

"So I was thinking that in our unique situation it would be to both of our best interests, given what we both have done and know about each other, to be able to invoke the marital privilege so that if one of the missions turns to shit we can't be compelled to testify against each other."

"You mean I wouldn't be able to turn state's evidence and sell you out to get a better deal for myself? I don't know. I like to keep my options open." She couldn't help but laugh then.

"Seriously. I think it's a good idea."

"So this is your marriage proposal? You are so romantic I could swoon."

He looked as if she had slapped him, stricken. She leaned over, hugged him, waited a minute and continued. "You know I adore you and would marry you in a heartbeat but there are some things you don't know. There is a good reason I can't do it. I'll tell you why some time."

"Why not now?"

Sydney went to the railing, put her hands on it and looked at nothing. "I have to work my way up to it."

6

How does one locate a hitman? That was Sydney's initial question when she set up her Human Pest Control business. In effect asking how anyone might find her if that type of service was needed. They're not in the Yellow Pages and couldn't very well advertise. Not being part of a mafia family meant she had no insider connections that could funnel business to her, so how could she break into the profession? The local bookstores carried paramilitary type magazines and had ads for mercenaries and protection services. Would this be where a person would start?

What about asking around in bars and making discreet inquiries? The problem with that was that the guy you finally found was probably going to be an undercover cop. The classifieds in the *Soldier of Fortune* type mag's and websites didn't reveal what she was looking for either. She assumed they would use some kind of code word to indicate the kind of jobs that would be undertaken but had to learn about that.

Research revealed that the easy to find hitman-for-hire websites were phony. Most were likely set up by kids and jokesters. Some even had price lists and an address where to send the cash. She was positive these were fake and wondered how many gullible people actually sent money to the websites. Could be a good scam, she thought. Would the person who sent the money complain to the authorities that the hitman he had tried to hire had stiffed him? But as she dug deeper she found there was more available on the internet than what could be found on Google, Yahoo, or Bing.

There was a hidden internet where one could procure anything from drugs to guns to—yes, hitmen. It was tricky and utilized a special download involving Tor, a site program that made your internet searches anonymous and invisible. There were clear instructions available though so that with a lot of time and some work even a non-expert computer user could configure a computer to use the program. Sydney's site was searchable on Tor, despite being blocked on some of the primary search engines.

When she set up the Human Pest Control website she had several critical criteria. HumanPestControl.com would also have to guarantee complete anonymity. The risk from the client standpoint was that they would pay money and nothing would be done. The client would then have no recourse and no way to complain. So she structured the site to make it clear that only certain jobs would be undertaken and only after careful research.

When investigating a potential assignment she would send the client bits and pieces of data to assure them she was working on the case and legitimate. And as a way of giving a potential client some level of comfort she asked for only half the fee up front and half on completion. If the job could not be completed through no fault of her own, like for instance the mark gets sent to prison, no more money was due. The website language reiterated the safety in the cloaking promised by the Tor program so that a client felt safe.

It took three months before she got a legitimate request for help that she felt fit her parameters. At the time she was living in Manhattan, working as a gallery assistant, and sharing space with Marta, a lesbian law student who wanted a roommate, not a lover. That relationship lasted until Marta found "the one" and Sydney was asked to move out. The first assignment hadn't paid much, but it was low impact and successful.

When Sydney first started the business, she expected most of the requests for help to be for violent sorts of acts. Not so much, though she did get them. A twelve-year-old playground bully was her first victim. It was the first time she had used a disguise and the first time she had taken money to solve a problem. This was one of the toughest kinds of cases to solve. The bully was a minor, so criminal charges would have little effect. She couldn't just go beat the crap out of the kid or kill him either—she had to make the remedy somewhat equal to the crime.

The solution she settled on was a mixture of fear and shame. She wanted to help the boy and the mother, but it wasn't easy.

A bully can be a serious problem. In this case, her client's son Todd was being pushed around at school. The typical things: stealing his lunch money, throwing his books over the fence, tripping him in the hallway, punching him when no one was looking. Mom had tried everything. She talked to the principal first, who said he would look into it but did nothing. The bully's parents were called to the office but the boy denied everything and the parents threatened to sue. Then, of course, the bully went after poor Todd even more aggressively.

Mom had gone to a lawyer who sent letters to the school and the parents but explained that without some sort of evidence, such as an injury witnessed by someone else, there was nothing to be done. The poor child was now refusing to go to school, was wetting the bed and the parents were taking him to a shrink. Mom was frantic. The boy's father was no help, offering to teach him to box and stand up like a man. There were no private schools in the area, so mom contacted Sydney through the website.

This was one of the toughest kinds of cases to solve.

The bully was a minor, so criminal charges would have little effect. She couldn't just go beat the crap out of the kid or kill him either—she had to make the remedy somewhat equal to the crime. Mom had provided her with a photo of the kid from the school yearbook (she was astounded that a seventh-grade class had a yearbook) and the names of his parents so he was easy to find.

Sydney knew that bullying was a huge issue and the best answer would have been a wholesale societal change. But she had one case and couldn't solve the problem by enrolling the bully in therapy or discussing the issue with the parents, teachers, and children in a forum setting. Hers was an effective but brutal solution that left no one injured and the bully's victim better off.

She had done some surveillance, took some pictures, did a little research and was ready to execute her plan. On a Monday morning Sydney stopped by Target and picked up a blond wig, some jogging pants and top with a white blouse and athletic shoes—mom attire—and bought a cheap stroller, a life size baby doll whom she named Cindy and wrapped it in a pink child's blanket. Then she put the costume on and went to the school.

Pushing the stroller down the sidewalk, she stopped from time-to-time to adjust Cindy's blanket and talk to her, hoping no other mothers came by. The playground at the middle school was fenced on the sidewalk side but open on the end, so she went in. Tommy was playing with other kids but not beating anyone up at the moment.

After a while she managed to find him alone and walked over. A mom with a stroller is pretty unthreatening.

"Tommy?" Sydney asked as she approached him. He stopped and looked at her as she got closer.

"You are Tommy Manville, aren't you?"

"Yeah." He was curious, didn't recognize her, but she did know his name so that was something. And she was not a sleazy guy in shades and a dirty baseball cap so he wasn't afraid—yet.

"Let's sit for a minute," she said pointing to some bleachers nearby. The rest of the kids were some distance away. "I feel a little dizzy from the sun. Oh. I'm a friend of your mother, and I have a message for you. You can call me Mrs. Kravitz."

"Okay, Mrs. Kravitz." He followed her and the stroller and they sat on the bottom bench of the bleachers. He was not the big kid that she had imagined, and was about the same size as her client's child.

"Okay. I want you to look me in the eye and listen very carefully." He turned and did.

"I am not your friend and I am not your mother's friend. I know exactly what has been going on with you and Todd. I'm not here to listen to you deny anything because we both know what's true"

He sneered, "What are you, his aunt or something?"

Sydney reached over and grabbed his wrist. He tried to pull away, but her training had taught her certain pressure points which can be incredibly painful if applied correctly. She just gave him a little taste. He tried to pull away but her grip was vice-like.

"Don't yell out. It will only hurt worse. I'm not going to kill you or anything. Just listen. This is only going to take a minute, then I'll let you go. Here's the deal. You leave Todd alone. That's it. You don't have to apologize or be his friend— just pretend he's invisible and the problem is solved and you will never see me again."

"You can't tell me what to do. I'll tell my dad and you'll be in for it." He looked around for help. The rest of the kids were leaving the playground with the supervisors. Sydney gave him another little touch of pain.

"Pay attention. I am not anyone your mother or dad knows and neither does Todd's mother. I don't have a baby, I just found this one, borrowed it, you might say..." she kicked the stroller and it nearly tipped over. "I took the kid from the mall to use for cover. I gave it a pill to keep it quiet. I'm going to give the little brat back when I'm done with you. God I hate kids.

"The thing is that if I hear that Todd has been hurt, that he is being harassed, or that he won't go to school, I'm going to blame you. I don't care whether you were the one that did it or not. So you should see that others don't bother him. If anything happens to him I'll assume you were responsible and I'll come see you again. You won't know when. You won't know who to look for because I won't look like this next time. It might be in the mall, or while you're riding your bike, or even while you're playing with your computer in the family room in your basement." She leaned over and whispered in his ear. "I know what else you do down there too. I have pictures I don't think your mom and dad would want to see. I can put these on the internet too. You wouldn't like that." She pulled photos from her pocket she had taken of him through the basement window and let him glance at them. He was playing with something but it wasn't his computer. "But the physical punishment will be worse. You will see what real pain can be. I don't think you'll like it." She squeezed again.

Throughout the talk Tommy had started to break down and was now crying. He had stopped trying to squirm away since her grip caused pain when he moved.

"Now I'm going to go. I want you to sit right here until I am out of sight. Remember though that if you cause Todd any trouble, you will pay for it. If you want to take a chance on telling your dad, just remember that I can hurt him too. So be a good boy, leave Todd alone from now on, and all will be well. Wait here until you can't see me anymore."

She let him go, pushed the stroller leisurely back the way she had come, waving to Tommy from the sidewalk. He waved back automatically. Then she went home after dumping her disguise, the stroller, and Cindy into a dumpster.

Todd's Mom emailed a couple of weeks later saying she was sending the other half of the fee and thanked Sydney.

The first case had come out great from Sydney's perspective. She got paid, stopped a bully, and made Todd's life happier. Tommy might have a few nightmares, but she thought he deserved them and would probably think twice before pushing other kids around again. If only they were all that simple.

It was her first success, if you didn't count avenging the death of her brother.

7

Oscar and Sydney worked and lived together for a year before she revealed her pest control business to him. That revelation had nearly ended the relationship and it was only when she was instrumental in saving the life of Oscar's best friend Roy that he finally accepted her role as an avenger. He had seen her in action and knew many of the things she had done but still found it hard to believe when he looked at her. She just didn't fit his stereotyped image of a hitwoman. But then what should such a person look like?

The things she did seemed to her to be justified and her reasoning was rational and sound. She wasn't circumventing the law, she said, she was aiding it. A free-lance prosecutor, judge, and jury. When a glitch occurred and the guilty went unpunished, she was there to make things right. But he still worried about mistakes that they might have made. Especially this last one when she killed Earl Santiago. He had no reason to suspect problems. Sydney was very careful, but he was concerned something could lead the police to them.

"If I'm not worried you shouldn't be either," Sydney told him as they worked in the gallery. "My security procedures are excellent. Nothing went wrong and the cops are writing Earl off as a terrific and public-friendly accident."

"I know all that," Oscar said. "And it's not that I doubt you, it's just that you're putting yourself in situations where you could get hurt and I have no way to help you. I need to assist if there's a next time."

"Will your conscience let you do that? I killed someone. A bad guy to be sure, but still a formerly living human being."

"I killed someone once myself. You might remember the scenario since you were there," Oscar said.

"But not face-to-face with a weapon. You ran your car into a boat to save me and it happened that the perp was on the boat when it exploded. I appreciated that, but it's a lot different when it's one-on-one. Some people have nightmares. Or they freeze and end up getting killed themselves."

"It didn't bother me. Justice served as you say." Oscar dropped onto a bench for a breather. This was the time when he would have had a cigarette back when he smoked.

"To me the best way to cope is business as usual," Sydney said. "Once it's over none of it happened as far as I'm concerned. I put all that sort of thing, all the details, all the things I did, in a separate room in my brain and never open the door."

They hadn't discussed Oscar's marriage idea again and he thought it was her move on that front.

Oscar tried to return to normal and was reviewing submissions of artwork for an upcoming juried show he was sponsoring at the gallery. Nowadays the entries were all digital and were reviewed on the computer; either downloaded images that artists had submitted online or by viewing their digitized photos from CD's and DVD's. It used to be done with slides and slide projectors in darkened rooms but times change.

"What if you accept something for the show and it sucks when it gets here?" Sydney said.

"To counteract that I put a little fine print on the entry forms saying we make the final decisions based on the work itself. If it's marginal I'll just hang it in the hallway instead of the main gallery and hope they don't come visit. If it's crap I'll leave it in the shipping crate to return to the artist when the show closes."

"Oh, yeah. Your lawyer training coming out. Do they

have to have their signatures notarized and swear under oath?"

"You're so cute when you're being a smart ass. Anyway, I like this final group so if you wouldn't mind emailing the acceptances and rejections I would appreciate it."

"Why don't you take the time to learn more about the computer so I don't have to do everything?" Sydney stood and turned off the monitor.

"I'm spending all my spare time mastering my new smart phone with all the gadgets and apps that I can find, trying to keep up with you. The technological world is my Apple, or at least I'm working at it. That's when I'm not being a secret agent's sidekick." Oscar said.

Earl the Cannibal's death was all over the news. Even CNN had it on the national broadcast and the *New York Times* had a small print and longer online story about the bizarre accidental death of the notorious alleged killer. A side article warned of the dangers of common household chemicals. Sydney could have written the article herself. She said she had another half-dozen recipes for death and destruction using ingredients from any local hardware and grocery.

Sydney and Oscar didn't discuss Earl's case again except for her acknowledgment that it had gone well. They had an understanding to keep looking ahead, not behind. She had told him early on that when she decided to take a life it had to be deserved. This was not a decision she made lightly. Every time she did it she was also avenging her brother.

After sending out the emails Sydney checked her Pest Control site one more time for the day. She had sent instructions for the second-half payment for the Earl job via another text from a safe phone and had confirmed that the money was now in hand. The guy had taken three days to pay, so she was almost ready to make him the next victim, but he had come through.

The other new request was intriguing and fit her parameters. Justice not served. Another severe case that begged for revenge. She would look into that one as well.

8

The new case was looking like a keeper. The target was a man again—most of them were. But he wasn't a violent killer or child abuser. It was white collar crime. A con-man and scammer taking a little here and there from volumes of people. The schemes the guy ran preyed not on wealthy investors, but on the elderly and desperately poor who were trusting and needy but who could ill afford any losses. So was death the appropriate answer in this case? Sydney dug deeper since killing him seemed extreme. If lethal force was justified, the case would require much more careful planning and investigation, and a higher fee due to the risk and potential penalty if caught.

Charles "Mo" Atwood ran a boiler room under various corporate fronts using several cons, old and new. His team of telephone callers sometimes pretended to be distant relatives, neighbors, or church friends who were in trouble. They needed money for personal disasters, like their wallet being stolen and they needed a hotel room or car repairs while on vacation. Or bail money for a great-grandchild.

The telephone operators worked off sophisticated scripts with prewritten answers to any objection a patsy might ask. The money request might start at fifty-dollars, or a hundred, and if the money was wired via Western Union as requested, there would be a call for more. The promise to pay it back in a week was usually made, offering interest.

Facebook provided much of the personal information Mo needed to make the fake pleas for help seem legitimate. A lot of people didn't keep their personal information private so it was easy to find the family names, when they were taking vacations and where, the location of summer homes, birthdays, illnesses; all information that could be used to manipulate the victims.

One scam that Sydney thought everyone had heard of was the payment of too much money for an item for sale on one of the websites such as EBay or Craigslist. Mo's people would make the deal for some expensive item, like a car or antiques, and would send a check for more than the agreed price. A mistake, the seller thought, who would then contact the buyer to return the overpayment. Mo's people would ask the seller to send the overpayment via Western Union, so as not to hold up delivery of the item.

They would often sweeten the deal by offering a bonus for the seller's inconvenience. Of course the original check, though it looked like a cashier's check, was no good, but since it was from an out of country bank the system took several days to recognize it. By then the victim had sent the overpayment back. It was too late to do anything once the money was picked up by the buyer and by the time the police investigated and decided to get involved all communication links had changed. Sometimes the victims even shipped the item that had been purchased before they discovered the bounced check. Even with broad publicity coverage of these scams, people still fell for them. Sydney had found most people were basically trustworthy and wanted to think everyone else acted the same way. So the age-old cons continued.

A one-time rip-off could be weathered by most people but Mo and his people didn't stop there. If they found a particularly susceptible victim they kept after him or her. Mo even used the old scheme originated in Nigeria. The inheritance scam. In order to get the phony inheritance transferred to the heir, cash was requested to cover attorney or government fees, they apologized and explained. It might be several hundred dollars. A lot of money to the patsy, but worth it to get a two hundred thousand dollar inheritance.

So the victim paid and paid again and again when new problems arose until the victim was completely tapped out. Some of the suckers even stole the needed money from their employers, thinking they would pay it back when the inheritance came through. There was too much invested to stop now. They would often end up bankrupt or in prison. Mo was a sociopathic son of a bitch.

If the prosecutors eventually closed in, Mo took off, sometimes just to a different building in the same city, taking his employees and telephone equipment with him and started the same scam over under a different company name. He was rarely out of business for more than a few days. He had previous criminal cases against him that he had beaten since the authorities were unable to tie him directly to ownership of the businesses, and had actually been convicted on one case, but the penalty in that was just a fine, so no problem. The civil lawsuits that were justified were rarely filed since no lawyer would take the cases on contingency and the clients couldn't afford their hourly rates.

At first glance it didn't look like her kind of case. But the client and her research gave a lot of details. Two of the victims of the fraud had committed suicide. There were lost homes, divorces. And it seemed the police and authorities weren't highly motivated to stop him. Some of Mo's victims were living on the edge to begin with and only one or two week's pay away from living on the street. To them it was deadly serious.

Even had Mo been prosecuted there was little like-lihood of anyone getting money back. And given the nature of sentencing for this type of crime, if he went to prison at all it would be a minimum security place nicer than the homes of most of his victims.

So people were hurt. Some had died. Others ruined financially or in jail. No one would help. Mo would not go to jail for long even if caught. There was no way to restore the money people had lost, and stopping him seemed the only solution.

So Sydney would erase him.

She had been given Mo's email contact information, a possible stopover he was making and the place he had them send the Western Union payments, though that was little help. The way it worked was that a money recipient at Western Union could pick up the payola at any office, anywhere in the world. Western Union had hundreds of thousands of locations worldwide, making a stakeout impossible.

The uncomfortable part of the job was the client who requested the hit. It was the same guy that had paid to have Earl the Cannibal killed. Pastor Luke. She had to find out what was up. Maybe the guy was on some vendetta to use her to help bring justice to the world, but maybe it was something else. Something didn't smell right here.

The other problem was that he had sent her a fifty thousand dollar retainer to the wire transfer address he had used before without her even asking for it. She would be happy to keep it and do nothing. What would he be able to do? But that plan had gone bad on her in the past. She needed more information.

Further research verified all the bad that Mo Atwood had done and that he seemed to be beyond justice. No high-profile people had been hurt by him and as far as the police, prosecutors, and postal service inspectors were concerned he was not a priority. So far so good for him. But not for long.

More investigation of Pastor Luke did not reveal any connection with Mo, just as there had been no connection with

Earl. He seemed to be genuinely interested on some personal level to see that this guy was brought to justice. It still seemed strange that he would put up so much money without having a personal reason, but sometimes there really are people with more money than sense.

Luke had no home address for Atwood, but advised that he knew that Mo would be attending a fundraiser at an exclusive country club in Vero Beach the following Friday and planned on staying with friends on the grounds. It was only ninety miles north of West Palm, thankfully. Just five days to prepare, and Sydney had no plan.

She checked the country club website and it gave details of the event. It was a local bar association function to raise campaign funds for a state Supreme Court judge running for re-election. In Florida Supreme Court judges could be voted out of office, but not into office, which Sydney found odd. The vote would be whether the judge should or should not retain her seat. If the voters said not, then the governor would appoint a replacement who would six years later be subject to the same voting procedure.

Getting into the event would be difficult, since it was by invitation and in a private club. She couldn't sneak in, just show up, or pretend to be a caterer since everything was done in-house. And the fancy clubhouse sat in the center of one hundred-sixty acres, all surrounded by swamp and fence, so it wasn't even visible from the road. The only entrances were through two manned gates, one for members and the other a service entrance. Both would require some kind of pass or a name on a list to get in. She could slog through the swamp but it was difficult, dangerous, and unpleasant. There were alligators, giant Burmese Pythons, spiders, and poisonous snakes out there that she did not want to have to deal with unless she was positive Mo would be there when she arrived.

Mo was supposed to be staying on the grounds, most likely at the home of one of the club members, many of whom lived on their estates in the golf course community. But she had no way to confirm that, and didn't trust the information Luke was going to provide enough to stake her life on it. So Mo could be staying anywhere, like in one of the many multi-million dollar gated communities dotting the oceanfront in that area.

If she could get inside the reception legitimately as a guest, there might be a way to at least get more information on his office or home location. Or confirm where he was staying on the grounds. Maybe there would even be an opportunity to take care of him on the spot. She doubted there would be any bodyguards beyond the gatekeeper, but nowadays a lot of paranoid people had taken to carrying concealed weapons. Like herself for instance.

She had even seen some ladies at a gun show picking out pink and pastel blue .25 caliber pocket pistols that fit nicely into their handbags. She didn't want to get into a showdown gun battle with the rich in their evening attire. The image it brought to mind amused her, imagining a well-coiffed trophy wife whipping up her dress and pulling out a pink gun from a holster strapped to her thigh.

The event was about lawyers and judges so maybe Oscar would have some ideas. She found him in his studio sculpting a figure of a female nude in clay. It was about one-fourth scale and on his adjustable sculpture stand. He was not wearing the apron she had bought him to protect his clothes and had red clay wiped on his pants and shirt.

A model Sydney had never seen before was posing nude, in position on a raised platform in front of him. A wall of mirrors behind her gave him a view of her front and back. She saw Sydney first, but didn't move.

"Hi there," she said.

"Hi back," Sydney answered, and went back to her room, not wanting to bother Oscar right then. She was a bit annoyed, not because of the model, Oscar had been hiring nude models for years and in fact Sydney regularly modeled for him, but she didn't like being surprised like that. Okay, maybe deep down she was a bit jealous.

Oscar came in about fifteen minutes later, wiping his hands on his shirt.

"What's up?"

"Nothing. I just wanted to talk to you."

"You could have stayed. You've seen me work before."

"Sorry. It shouldn't be uncomfortable for me but it is. You don't get it, but some of these women would do more than just model if you asked. I could smell that one after you."

"I do get it. And I don't ask. I already have you, which is a lot. Anyway, what do you need?"

She explained the situation with the country club fundraiser.

"Who's the candidate?" He sat on the edge of her computer desk.

"Her honor, Sylvia Pocholi."

"I know her. Well, we're not friends or anything, but before she was appointed judge she was in private practice and we were on opposite sides of several divorce cases. A back-stabber more interested in winning the case than helping the client. Can't trust her. But she wants contributions so maybe I could get invited. Bring you as a guest. I'll have to get my tux cleaned and pressed and buy you an evening dress."

"I can dress myself, thank you. Getting me in there would be enough help. Let me know as soon as possible so I can make plans."

"We're not going in or out with guns blazing, I hope. Country club people don't like that sort of thing."

"You know I'm usually more discreet. And this is just a fishing expedition. Besides, they'll love you when you pop for a big contribution."

"I don't even like the woman. Why would I contribute?"

"I'm supplying the cash. It's a business expense for me and takes any suspicion off. I just need to get inside legitimately."

"Then I'll see what I can do. Asking to be invited so I can give her money should get me an easy ticket."

By Wednesday he had secured the invitation. On Thursday an email came in from Pastor Luke. He had an address where Mo would be staying and it was on the country club grounds. So now the serious planning began. She looked up the address and got the names of Mo's hosts, Bruce and Sherry Lindemann. He was—no surprise—a hedge fund manager. Using Google Earth she got an aerial and street view of the property.

The main house was on the golf course and a separate guest house was closer to the winding drive through the subdivision. Both buildings were two stories and surrounded more by paving stones than grass. There were no fences around the individual estates. It was highly likely there was a security force of at least two guards in the complex at all times. One would be on the gate and there would probably be a rover, driving around the streets with no fixed schedule. Some of them used golf carts, others cars. She would know more before she arrived.

9

Pheasant Ridge Country Club is an ultra-exclusive residential and golf facility a few miles west of Vero Beach. In addition to the eighteen championship golf holes, other amenities included a social club, pool, spa, private beach and restaurant on the Atlantic as well as a yacht basin on the Intracoastal Waterway. The homes, as Sydney had found, all included adjacent guest cottages that anywhere else would be considered mansions in their own right.

A few days later Oscar and Sydney drove up to the entrance gate in Oscar's vintage 1965 Mustang, using some of his precious miles on the low-mileage collector car. They had left the top up in deference to Sydney's concern about her hair staying in place. Oscar teased her about her appearance since she typically wore tight T-shirts and black Levi's or her motorcycle leathers if using her Harley. She had replaced her normal black eye shadow and lipstick with a look more like what she thought the society types would be wearing and had removed two of her three sets of earrings and all her piercing jewelry.

"I clean up okay," she said, a little miffed after his ribbing. She had strapped a razor-sharp folding ceramic knife to her inside right thigh with elastic—just in case. Her ankle-length red dress was cut low in the front, but not so low as to not be tasteful. She didn't want to look slutty, just sophisticated. The long auburn wig covered her black hair that she had pinned down. She had affixed a believable temporary tattoo of a small red heart to the outside of her left wrist and put in green contacts. She didn't mention to Oscar that she had made the dress herself and had designed it to help carry out the mission if the opportunity arose.

Oscar wore the ubiquitous black tux with black tie and had no weapons on him, though he normally kept a nine-millimeter in the glove box. He had finally given in and got a concealed weapons permit from the state after getting in trouble for not possessing one recently, but didn't plan on carrying the gun to the party. In the trunk was a kit of supplies in the event she was able to slip away and take care of Mo at his guest house. Maybe he would fall off a second story balcony after drinking too much. If he had a balcony. It was hard to tell from the Google Earth satellite imagery.

She had several alternate plans if she could confirm his staying at his host's address. She carried a small clutch bag of the kind most women carried for things like lipstick and cab fare. Sydney's bag contained those, but also more lethal supplies.

The guard checked Oscar's name off the list and asked the name of his guest. She leaned over, smiled, and said "Louise Nevils. And yours?" The guard blinked, pointed to his chrome name tag and said, "Arnie. Nice to meet you." He wrote the name on his pad and as if by magic the gate lifted and they went through.

"Remote control on his belt," said Sydney automatically.

"Louise?"

"I didn't want to use my secret identity. Louise is just as real as far as paperwork is concerned. It will check out. She even has a passport."

They rolled up the drive, three hundred yards of two-lane brick pavers flanked by towering royal palms winding up to the front of the two-story limestone clubhouse. They pulled up under the portico. A team of valets descended on the car, helping them out and driving the Mustang away. Oscar was reluctant to let them have it and Sydney patted his arm sympathetically. At Sydney's suggestion he gave them only the ignition key. The older Mustangs had separate keys for the trunk and ignition.

They had to walk through a portable metal scanner which seemed the only security. It was set low so as not to be set off by a belt buckle or Rolex and nobody was checking purses. The security seemed more for show than anything else. The ceramic knife would not have shown up anyway. They entered a two-story foyer with a chandelier the size of a grand piano and were greeted at the door by a young woman who provided them with small brass pins with their names already printed on them. Apparently the guard had called ahead and they had some computer process to do the printing. Pretty upscale and slick.

"A lot classier than the paper stick-on ones that say 'Hi, My Name is _____" Oscar said.

"Yeah. Look around, Oscar. Notice anything?" They stood just inside the doorway to the ballroom.

"Lots of people in fancy dresses and tuxedos. A couple of white dinner jackets, wait staff with trays of drinks and hors d'oeuvre's."

"No, you guy, you. The women. The dresses. Everybody but me is wearing pastels."

"Red suits you. Besides, you're the best looking woman here."

"Yeah, right. The women that aren't eighty look like these guys bought them from an ad in the back of the *Sports Illustrated* swimsuit issue. Whole lot of silicone here. Keep your eye out for Mo. I may need to cozy up to him."

"I have to find Sylvia. Make an introduction for you.

But they'll probably find me first, not wanting me to forget the campaign contribution."

"I'm sure that's taken care of very discreetly by an underling. Don't worry, they won't forget."

A string-quartet played in one corner of the ball room. The ceiling was high with three identical crystal chandeliers providing the light. Across the room a wall of glass looked out over the golf course lit by the patio lights. They picked up drinks, talked party talk to an elderly couple and laughed pleasantly while Sydney scanned the crowd.

Where was Mo? She had a description and had seen a small online photo but there had to be fifty white men here that could fit the description. Grey hair, heavy tan, medium height and all wearing the same costume. So she had to mingle. She nudged Oscar and he wandered off in another direction looking at name tags.

There was a dance area to one side of the room. Sydney couldn't see dancing to a string quartet. They were clearly used to giving recitals rather than acting as a dance band, but the members did their best to adapt. She lost Oscar and strolled through the crowd sipping the original glass of white wine she had been offered. The all-too-familiar chardonnay, but she drank a little of it anyway since, as Oscar said, the best wine you could have was what was available. People smiled, trying to recognize her, but she didn't stop to talk until someone backed into her. It was the judge candidate, Sylvia Pocholi. She turned and they were face-to-face.

"Hello, I don't believe we've met." Sylvia extended her hand and smiled widely. She was holding a clear drink, either vodka or soda. Sydney decided soda.

"Louise Nevils. It's a pleasure." Sydney shook her hand and the judge pulled her gently to the side, moving her along. She had apparently seen someone with a bigger checkbook on the horizon. "Have a nice time." She was already holding her hand out to someone else.

Sydney finally made the circle back toward the entrance when she caught up to Oscar.

"Let's dance," he said.

"You don't dance unless you're drunk." But she placed her glass on the tray of a waitperson and grabbed Oscar's arm.

"You won't believe the men's room in this place." He talked quietly in her ear, holding her close.

"Yeah? What?"

"I went out to the hallway and I guess I missed the one for the ballroom and ended up at the men's locker room for the golf club. Big double oak doors. Heavy carpet. There's a full bar in there, but not staffed tonight. But the main thing is it's huge and has these dioramas, like you'd see in a museum."

"Dioramas? You mean like an Indian village?"

"No. Stuffed wild animals. Whoever set this place up must be a big game hunter. There's a ten-foot tall stuffed grizzly bear standing on its hind legs with its teeth bared like it's about to eat you standing in the center of the room amidst a pile of rocks. Impressive as hell. Then next to the bar is another scene set up with a full size African lion, mane and all. Plus animal heads on the walls, gazelles, buffalo, big horn sheep, stuffed birds. It's like a dead zoo."

"Maybe I'll use the men's so I can see. If I find Mo maybe we could lure him in there, finish him off and blame it on the bear. I would be willing to bet the women's locker room isn't so lavish. They probably didn't even let women play here twenty years ago."

"Twenty years ago this was a grapefruit grove."

Sydney pulled Oscar around one-hundred eighty degrees. "Look straight ahead. See the big guy in the white suit?"

"Yes. So?"

"It's my client, Pastor Luke Anger. I recognize him from his website. What the hell does he think he's doing here?"

"Watching his investment? Maybe hoping to see Mo get taken out? Or perhaps he was planning on attending all along and that's why he knew Mo would be here."

"This is totally inappropriate. But he doesn't know who I am or even that I'm a woman so probably no danger to me, but it's unnerving."

"We can leave and call it off if you want."

"No. Let's just see how it plays out."

Just then Sydney spotted the Charles Mo Atwood lapel pin near them, the wearer not dancing, but talking to another man and woman. She pointed him out to Oscar, then waited for an opportunity to approach. Mo was holding a mixed drink and gulped it down as he talked. Finally the couple moved on and Sydney moved in after taking a clear envelope not much bigger than her thumb from her bag and palming it. Magic tricks and sleight of hand had been one of her favorite pastimes as a child, before the bad stuff happened. But she still remembered a few things.

She walked quickly toward him, looking another way, but very sure of where he was. She lifted her arm, as if she had seen someone or remembered something and turned sharply, bumping him hard in a way that knocked his drink from his hand. It was mostly empty but the glass bounced on the hardwood floor and skittered away, not breaking. The staff was on it immediately.

"Oh, my. I am so sorry," she said, putting her hand on his forearm that had been holding the glass and which was still perpendicular to him.

"Hey, no problem. I can get more. Have we met?"

"I haven't had the pleasure but I guess we have now. I'm Louise." She extended her hand. The one without the envelope.

"Charles Atwood. Friends call me Mo." His hand was damp and soft which Sydney found creepy, but gave him her best smile.

"Are you a friend of the judge?" Sydney asked, beating him to it.

"No, but I have friends who know her and I'm one of those who get invited to these kind of things since I support the party."

"The party? Oh, you mean the political party. Yes. I know what you mean. I wonder if I'll be invited back if I don't contribute sufficiently? Are you staying here on the grounds?"

"Yeah. With the Lindemanns in their guest house. Do you know them? But just for the night. Got to get back to work tomorrow."

Very productive small talk. He was staying at the address Luke had provided. The house was actually within walking distance from the clubhouse if you cut across the tenth fairway. She thought this would work.

"Oh, I forgot about your drink. What was it?"

"Someone will be around. I'll doubt they're out of scotch."

"No. I insist. I see a server right over there. It was my fault. I'll be right back. You drink it neat, right? I didn't see any ice cubes bouncing across the floor."

"Right." He grinned, and Sydney imagined he was planning the evening with her.

She got the drink and no one noticed her dropping in the little clear envelope filled with white powder. The envelope and contents dissolved on contact with the alcohol. She stirred it with a little plastic straw and took it back to him.

"Here you are. Are you with someone?" She looked around.

"No one except you. Did you come alone?"

"I got an invitation from a friend so I came, but it's not really a date." She pointed to Oscar who was getting another glass of wine. "It was so nice to meet you, Mo. Perhaps we'll run into each other again some time."

"Ha. I'll watch my drink next time. But I would love to see you again. Call me." She took his proffered card. There was no address, just telephone numbers and email. But he was wrong. He wouldn't love their next meeting. She retreated to Oscar.

"What was that about? Is it a good idea to let the victim get to meet you like that?" Oscar handed her another glass. She didn't drink the first one and wouldn't this one either.

"He won't be around to testify against me. I added twenty milligrams of Xanax to his drink."

"You slipped him a mickey? I've always wanted to say that."

"It's not going to knock him out right away, but he's going to have a short evening. Combined with the alcohol he won't be staying up late partying with his hosts. My expectation is that he'll go to the guest house and turn in early. A normal dose of Xanax is two milligrams. If he somehow doesn't go to sleep his reflexes are going to be very much off, which will make him easy to handle. The only thing that could go wrong is if he passes out in the main house and they don't send him to the guest house. But that's unlikely."

"How are you going to get into the guest house?"

She pretended to sip the drink. "We're leaving soon. I'll slip out of the car outside the gate, scale the little wall and work my way through the swamp to the golf course. I know the layout from the aerial views I memorized. I'll be sure to say goodbye to Arnie on the way out just for the record so I have proof we left early. I'll just need some things from my bag in the trunk before I bail. I'll call you for pickup when I'm done, but it will be couple of hours. I have to wait for Mo to come home and settle in. The pastor didn't seem to take any notice of us, so I guess we're okay."

There were lights along the roadway leading out but the golf course was unlit. They slowed and Oscar stopped to be sure Arnie recognized them on the way out. They pulled over to the side of the road when they were out of sight of the guardhouse and popped the trunk. Sydney selected a few items, put them in a shoulder strap bag and left the rest of the stuff in the car. Oscar pulled away as she stepped into the shrubbery near the wall.

She stripped off her skirt. She had designed it so that it came off easily with Velcro strips. Underneath she was wearing a black body suit. The wig and skirt were left in the shrubbery to pick up on the way out. She pulled on a pair of knee-high vinyl boots, climbed the wall and slogged through the swampy area, trying to stay on firm ground and hoping that the snakes were asleep and the gators were staying near the ponds.

She stepped out on the edge of the golf course, near a tee. The shoulder bag contained an aerosol canister the size of a can of spray paint, a twenty-gallon black plastic garbage bag, a roll of duct tape, her cell phone, rubber gloves, and a small thirty-eight caliber revolver with an attached silencer that she hoped not to have to use. She pulled off the boots and stashed them for the return trip.

Other than the man-made hills on the golf course the terrain was flat. There was no wild indigenous vegetation.

Every tree, flower, bush, and blade of grass had been planned and planted. It was so artfully done that it had a natural flow and look. Finding the Lindemann estate was easy enough since she had seen the aerial view online and knew its location in relation to the golf course. She stayed away from the illuminated roadway and walked between the golf course and the rear of the adjacent properties, staying near the edge. It was after ten and there were no dog walkers out.

In this sort of neighborhood dogs were not allowed to be outside unattended so she didn't worry about barking. The house was two par-four holes away from where she started, and according to the tee markers a total of seven hundred seventy yards. Sydney didn't play golf so the holes seemed far apart. Lights shown through the windows on the upper and lower floors of the main house. Everyone hadn't turned in yet. She expected that wouldn't be true for Mo for long. She skirted around the house to get to the roadway, staying in shadows and behind trees as she approached the guest house.

Both buildings were done in an English Tudor style with cut stone and slate roofs. Very un-Florida like. There were no balconies on the upper floor, but the windows were large, at least seven feet high and mullioned. Probably cranked open, she thought, which would make it difficult to access them. No lights were on in the guest house. The plans for the guest house were not available but she had seen similar ones in her research. There would be two to three bedrooms upstairs. The size and opulence of the place indicated an elevator in both houses, which she would stay away from. Downstairs would be a half-bath, living room, dining area, and full-size kitchen. Sometimes the stairs were outside but in this case not. She looked carefully for security cameras or motion detectors on the guest house.

None visible, but there was a laser warning beam across

the driveway entrance which she assumed alerted the main house if someone entered the driveway. Not much security, but they all probably felt safe in the compound and probably had panic alarms inside to alert on-site guards if a problem arose. She settled in, sitting on the ground, invisible amidst the landscaping, waiting for everyone to arrive. It was a cocktail party, not dinner, so she expected it to break up within the hour.

One car drove in eighty minutes later. It stopped at the guest house and the driver got out and helped Mo to the door. He waved and the car drove on to the main house, going around back to where the garages were located. Lights went on in both buildings. Five minutes later the lights went off in the guest house.

After another thirty minutes sitting motionless there was no visible activity on the grounds. Fifty quick steps and she was on the side of the guest cottage facing away from the main residence. She walked around, looking for an entrance. There were two standard doors and a slider off a small patio. She considered trying the front door but it was in view of the main house.

The windows indeed did crank open from inside so were not an option unless she broke one. The exception was a small window near the kitchen area. She put on her black rubber gloves, removed her shoes and brought a small side table over from the patio to stand on and looked in. It was the downstairs half-bath and the window was a jalousie type, sliding up, and was screened and open. The window screen frame popped out easily with her ceramic knife. A normal sized un-athletic person would not have been able to get through the window. But Sydney was strong, limber, and small. She dropped onto the tile floor soundlessly with her bag and waited for indoor sounds. Nothing.

Mo hadn't fallen asleep on the couch. She crept up the stairs, staying to the sides since she had found that stair centers were the most likely spot to creak. There was a landing open to the downstairs living room and off that, three doors. Two would be bedrooms, the one in the middle likely a Jack-and-Jill bathroom. The one on her left was closest. She placed the bag on the floor, took out the knife, and opened door number one quickly but silently. Another thing she knew was that the slower you opened a door the more it would squeak. She doubted these folks would tolerate a squeaky door but she stuck to procedure.

There he was. Sprawled on the bed on his back, fully clothed except for his shoes, jacket, and tie. She stepped to the other bedroom and the bath. Both were empty. Mo was snoring softly when she went back to his room. The main house was visible from the windows and nothing was stirring but the lights were still on. She opened her kit and got out the aerosol can, plastic bag, and duct tape. The drugs and alcohol should have him totally knocked out and unresponsive. The drugs took an hour or two for full effect and would last till mid-morning.

But he wouldn't live that long.

Still careful, she poked him in the ankle with the tip of the knife through his sock. If not drugged he would have shot bolt upright. No reaction. She put the knife away and found the mouth of the garbage bag but didn't open it. With the top off the aerosol, she stuck it inside the bag with her hand on the release button and put her arm all the way in, holding the bag opening around her arm with the other hand. Then she pushed the button, inflating the bag with the gas. When it was full she carefully pulled out her arm and the can, holding the bag closed so that it resembled a black balloon. Then she put the bag over Mo's head and used the pull ties to close it around his neck.

The gas was argon. It has no smell and is heavier than air, an inert gas used for industrial purposes and readily available without permissions or licenses. It was often used to replace atmospheric air in-between double-pane windows since it contained no oxygen or moisture. Every welding supply carried it. There is more argon in the air than there is oxygen and when inhaled alone it displaces the oxygen in the lungs. Death occurs within minutes, yet there is no gasping for breath or discomfort felt. A slightly elevated heartbeat for a while and the person dies peacefully. Welders are warned to work with their argon gas-shielded wire-welders in ventilated areas to avoid being overcome.

If autopsied, argon doesn't show up in normal screening since it's a component of the body and of the air itself. There is no petechial hemorrhaging on the body—the redness around the eyes and mouth that could occur in normal oxygen deprivation suffocation where force is used. So the cause of death is always listed as unknown. Argon has been used in suicides but the only reason the coroner can name it as a cause of death is because the argon cylinder is always at the scene.

She could have used helium, which is even easier to get, but since it's lighter than air, administration to the victim is more difficult. Sydney had often wondered why those states with the death penalty didn't use argon in a gas chamber instead of the lethal injection of drugs that seemed so much more difficult and less reliable.

Mo seemed to have stopped breathing but to be sure she squeezed the gas out of the bag, refilled it, put it back over his head and waited another several minutes while she watched the main house. While waiting she put four Xanax tablets in his pants pocket as evidence for the police. Finding no pulse, she removed the bag, stowed all her equipment, and exited through the bathroom window, putting everything back exactly as she had found it. Twenty minutes later she had negotiated the swamp, climbed over the wall at the front corner of the property, located her things, and stood in the weeds at the side of the road texting Oscar the code word to pick her up.

10

With the latest job out of the way, Oscar and Sydney concentrated again on the upcoming gallery show. Oscar had gotten almost used to helping with Sydney's jobs and then resuming business as usual. If Sydney wasn't worried why should he be? Once again they didn't discuss the case. Oscar thought it might be avoidance but Sydney seemed to have erased it from her memory. He had participated this time in a small way, but she didn't share the details of how she had carried out the hit. She would if he asked. But he didn't. Deniability in case things went south.

All but one of the paintings had arrived. Oscar had hung most of them with Sydney offering advice on placement. Announcements had been sent out. There was promise of a review of the show in the *Palm Beach Post*, and a half-dozen press releases were sent via email.

"When did they say the review would run?" Sydney asked. She was reading a recipe and preparing something Oscar thought smelled Mexican. Different kinds of peppers, cheeses and meats were covering the small counter near the stove. Her hair was up in a ponytail and a large black apron kept whatever was frying from spattering her bare tummy above her shorts and below her half a T-shirt.

"I really pushed for a preview so the review itself would run before the opening. What drives me crazy is when they review the show after it's closed. What good does that do anybody?"

"You should pay for an ad. I think you get better attention if you're a paying customer."

"I lose enough money on the Rose Madder as it is. If we weren't living above the gallery and using it for office space the gallery would have shut down long ago."

It was true. But they both knew the gallery wasn't intended as a money maker. It was Oscar's love. His hobby, but it was not wise to call it that to his face. Truth was that the gallery was very important to the exhibiting artists who built up their resume's by being accepted for a group or one-person show, even if the sales weren't terrific. This was West Palm, not Palm Beach, and the big-time galleries were located across the bridge on the island. But Oscar was an artist himself and enjoyed the interaction with the other artists and gallery visitors.

Dinner turned out to be a Cuban dish. Ropa Vieja. A spicy shredded flank steak with vegetables in a tomato base. Kind of like Spanish beef stew. Oscar cooked only rudimentarily so this was an exotic meal to him. Sydney was no gourmet, but could follow a recipe well enough to impress the hell out of Oscar.

"So I was thinking," said Sydney between sips of her Corona Light, "that it might be fun if we went to this bonsai nursery they have out the other side of I-95. Like maybe tomorrow. I want to see what they've got. Supposed to be a lot of mature bonsai and the guy there teaches classes and has some starters for sale."

Oscar kept eating. "How long will you be gone?"

"Oscar?" Sydney set her beer down and stared at him. "You were married once, right?"

"Right." He got up to get himself another Corona, signaling if she wanted another one by waiving the bottle. She ignored him.

"So when your girlfriend asks you to go someplace with her, even though she knows it might not be your first choice, it has nothing to do with you or trying to please you. It's a call for bonding. A time to be together doing something she likes and hopes you might a little bit. A way of sharing her stuff with you. The best answer in that situation is 'that sounds like fun'. Get it?"

"God, you do sound like a wife, but yeah, that sounds like fun."

"Oh, never mind. No wonder you're divorced. And I want to talk about that wife idea."

"Okay, so why can't you marry me?"

Sydney hesitated, then forged ahead. "The thing is, Oscar, I'm already married."

Oscar dropped his fork.

"Tell me."

She turned to him. "It was a several years before I came to Florida. I was living in Manhattan. Living with a friend when I met Matthew. He didn't know what I did. I told him I worked in a gallery in Soho, which I did as my day job. He was a graduate student in archeology at NYU. I don't know how to explain it. I had never had a boyfriend and I found myself married after only knowing him six weeks. It was crazy."

"So where is he now?" Oscar patted his shirt pocket, forgetting that he had quit smoking.

"I don't know. I'm pretty sure he's dead." She stopped talking for a minute. Oscar waited. "He went off on a six week tour with some other students to Columbia. Studying ruins and all that crap. He quit texting me and I assumed he was somewhere there was no cell service. But he never came home. I was beside myself and did everything I could think of. The American Embassy, lawyers, private detectives. I even took all my savings and went down there myself. His return ticket was never used. The government's best guess was that he had been kidnapped or killed or both. There's a notorious and well supported rebel group that does that sort of thing but they usually ask for ransom. But no ransom demand in his case. After two years I finally had to accept it. I still check with the State Department periodically. But no news. It's been six years now. In my heart I know he's dead. So I've moved on. Stay busy. But now I have you and it's different. Deeper. But as far as getting married I don't know if I can do it legally. You're the lawyer. What can I do?" A tear streaked her cheek.

"What name did you marry under?"

"Oh. That could be another problem. It was an alias that I had to abandon when I came here. But maybe that means no one would know and we could just go ahead and do it, right?"

"No. We have to have the marriage legally airtight and not subject to challenge to take advantage of the legal protections. I'll think on it. Maybe an annulment. Or have him declared legally dead."

"Does it bother you that I was married before? It was a long time ago."

"No. I was married before, remember? What bothers me is that you didn't tell me. I thought we had an understanding."

"Sorry. I guess I'm so used to keeping secrets about so many things that I have a hard time opening up. And you said you didn't need to know my history."

"I meant your history vis-à-vis your super-hero job."

They left the next morning for the bonsai farm to be there at ten when there would be a lecture and demonstration.

The Tiny Tree Bonsai Nursery was off a sand road that ran along a drainage canal ten miles west of I-95. Literally in the sticks. The area had once been in the swamp of the Everglades before the area was drained in the twenties for citrus and sugar cane agriculture. There was a small sign near the road and the driveway turned into a rutted single lane that led through cabbage palms and palmettos to a single story ranch house dominated by the quarter-acre size greenhouse and barn area behind it. "Greenhouse" in southern Florida did not necessarily mean a fully glass-enclosed structure, although there were some like that, but was an area that was screened on the top, sides, and bottom to dilute the intense sun and keep down the weeds.

Rows of shelving, which were nothing more than planks laid across the top of concrete blocks, were covered with thousands of clay and plastic pots containing the bonsai specimens, none more than two-feet high. Along one side was a more solidly built area where mature and carefully tended bonsai were displayed. The entire inside was laced overhead with piping for watering the many plants.

Even in the screened areas the air was heavy with plant smell and humidity. In the places enclosed in glass or plastic it was like breathing water and you immediately broke out into a sweat stepping through the doorway. Sydney said she loved it. She had asked Oscar to bring his camera and directed which specimens she wanted photographed.

Oscar walked through the aisles looking at the different kinds of plants. They looked to him initially like scrawny bushes, something you might hoe out of your garden before they spread. But after a while he began to see what it was all about. It must be difficult to keep them tiny, hold back their growth, keep them alive, but still make them look like the original trees, only on a miniature scale. And many had hardly any soil so they must have to water them all the time. It took love. Then he looked at the display bonsai. Some had ages on them, as old as seventy-five years, and price tags, as much as twenty-five hundred dollars. Oscar began to be impressed.

"What do you think about this one?" She had gathered a half-dozen potted specimens and had them arranged in a row near the check-out counter. She was pointing at one.

"It looks kind of scrawny. Almost dead. Hardly any leaves. Are there bigger and healthier ones?"

"Scrawny and few leaves are an asset to a bonsai. We want the ones that have struggled but still live. Old looking, crinkly, crooked. That's what makes them interesting." She picked up one of her choices and showed him.

"The opposite of people. I get it."

The proprietor came by just then. He had an aging hippie look with long gray hair in a ponytail, tan rugged face, worn T-shirt and tattered bib overalls with a rainbow embroidered on the bib. A human bonsai.

"Got the ones you want?" He talked softly, a long-time smoker's hoarse whisper. Not necessarily cigarettes. He held out his hand to Sydney and shook with both of them.

"I am Ezekiel. This is my place. You are first timers?"

"Actually I have some bonsai but that's true. I just started collecting," Sydney said.

"Are you committed to the journey?"

"You mean to take care of them? Yes. I'm studying but there's so much to know. I read that you give classes."

"Yes. We have them for all levels and specialized classes on individual types of plants. Here we use primarily tropicals but some bring their northern species with them as they travel. Bonsai do not like living alone. I also offer classes on yoga and meditation. If you are spiritual we have non-denominational services periodically. In fact I have a wedding to do this afternoon over under the big pergola." He pointed toward the house.

Oscar nudged Sydney. "He does weddings."

They arrived home with four new plants. She talked about the trip the rest of the way back, but not about the former husband, apparently putting that subject in the same mental room where her missions were stored. She thanked him for his patience when they got back home. He actually hadn't minded it. But the one trip would last him a while. Oscar was intrigued and mystified by Sydney, if that was her real name. Maybe it was Louise. She seemed so normal at times. Yet could be so many different people. The Harley riding hard-ass. The methodical and ruthless killer.

But when she explained her reasons she sounded so rational and reasonable. Oscar had been in some scrapes himself and had been forced to shoot someone once, as well as defend Sydney once with a boat crash, causing the justifiable death of a bad guy. Now he was an accessory to murder but it didn't weigh on him. So he understood in a way how a person could become inured to violent acts once enough were committed—and if the person was totally convinced she or he had done the right thing.

He knew some of her history—maybe more than he wanted. Growing up and being on the street and on her own at seventeen did not lead to a normal childhood. After her parents died she had been exposed to violence early on and had been forced to learn how to protect herself.

The transition to protecting others, albeit for money, was not hard to understand, even if some didn't agree with it. So he helped with her missions at times just to keep tabs on her. She had saved his ass in the past and he would do anything to protect her even when she was putting herself in harm's way.

Oscar picked up a newspaper when they stopped for gas. The death of Charles Atwood from the day before yesterday was a mere mention in the middle of the second section. It was being called an unexplained death with the medical examiner's report pending. The paper described Mo not as the sleaze he was, but as a businessman who had generously donated to many worthy local causes.

"So far they haven't picked up on his death being a murder," Oscar said.

"That's the plan. Either unexplained death or accident. They can categorize it as murder if they want. I am careful enough that there should be nothing tying me to his death."

"I don't know. I still worry that they might catch up to you one of these days."

"Oscar, you have to look at the situation and the statistics. I have never been caught or even questioned by the police and the reason is that I'm pathologically careful. And you know I wouldn't put you in jeopardy. The fact is that nearly all homicides are done impulsively by someone consumed with anger or jealousy. The ones that are actually planned are few and far between. And considering all that, even including the sloppy ones and the ones where the killer confesses or is caught in the act, only about one-third of all the murders in this country are ever solved. So the odds of not being caught or even suspected are heavily on our side. And the statistics keep getting worse—or better from my perspective. Thirty years ago the statistics were reversed. More were solved than not."

"One-third? Wow. How do you know all this?"

"Just keeping up with industry news."

Two days later the story on Mo had changed. On the front page of the Post, but below the fold, the headlines screamed, *Cannibal Killer a Serial Killer*. Oscar read the article to Sydney while they had breakfast upstairs.

Information leaked to the Post has led to the police tying together three murders throughout the state that had previously been reported as accidental. The cause of death of the notorious Earl Santiago, referred to as the Earl the

Cannibal, which had been attributed to accidental inhalation of poisonous gas has now been changed to homicide. The killer reportedly leaves a single rose and a small bible at each crime scene."

"Single Rose and Bible?" Sydney said. "What's that about?"

Oscar continued reading.

Another recent death, that of Charles 'Mo' Atwood has been attributed to a serial killer. The death investigation had not been completed since no cause of death had been determined. He died at the exclusive Pheasant Ridge Country Club in Vero Beach. just hours after attending a fundraiser for Judge Sylvia Pocholi of the Florida Supreme Court. A rose and bible were left near the house where he died leading the authorities to reexamine his autopsy.

A third murder which preceded the other two has also been tied to the so called Rose Bible Killer. A fifteen year-old boy in the Orlando area whose name has been withheld was asphyxiated. Death by self-induced auto-erotic asphyxiation was the initial cause of death but that has been changed to probable homicide based on the information received from a review of the autopsy and the presence of a rose and bible at the crime scene.

The article went on, detailing as much as the reporters had found out about the victims and the prior reporting on their deaths.

"This is serious. Someone is setting us up." Sydney took the paper and re-read it.

"Who is this other victim? It wasn't one of your hits so what's going on?" Oscar was pacing with his half-empty coffee cup.

"It looks to me like someone, maybe this Pastor Luke, is trying to pin the first murder on me because he or someone he's helping killed the first victim. Or maybe he had someone else kill victim one for his own reasons and wants to make it a serial killing to obfuscate things."

"What about the bibles and roses? He would have had to have known when the deaths were to occur to plant them and would have had to be on the scene before the bodies were discovered," Oscar said.

"He knew all that. I'm afraid Pastor Luke knows more than he should. So what do we do? Anything? Something? Nothing? Run? Kill him?"

"As you said, there should be no direct evidence tying us to any of the deaths. But we don't know what this Luke guy is up to or how he might try to implicate us. I think we have to solve the murder of the first victim to die—the one we didn't kill—to know for sure whom we are dealing with and then figure out how best to neutralize the danger that killer may pose to us."

"Doing nothing at all is sometimes the best course of action in solving a problem. Things often resolve themselves if you wait," Sydney said.

"But not this time. We can't wait and hope the police don't show up at the door." Oscar set his coffee cup down on the counter too hard, shattering the cup and spraying coffee.

"You're right," Sydney said. "Action. I'm not going to be somebody's serial killer by proxy."

PART TWO

1

They made their plan while having lunch at a water-front restaurant downtown. The first murder had been committed in Orlando so that was the logical place to start. They would get as much information as possible on the death of the victim and then begin an on-site investigation.

As they headed back to the gallery and were a half-block away they noticed a car parked at the curb out front. It was a dark-colored Mercury four-door with a spotlight mounted on the driver's-side door and two passengers in the front seats. They didn't need to tell each other it was an obvious unmarked police car.

Oscar turned right down the one-lane alley flanking the building to his parking area in the rear, driving under a row of sagging orange trees to the carport and near the rear entrance. Sydney got out and went to the rear door of the building.

"I have no desire to talk to the police and odds are they're here to see you anyway. If they ask about Louise give them this number." She pulled a store receipt from her pocket and wrote the number down. Oscar memorized it and gave the paper back. "It's the number of one of my unused burn phones. On the other hand if they ask about Sydney Simone, your roommate, that would be okay. Tell the truth except for the part about me also being Louise."

"You're probably right. It's the police, but no worries. It has to be about Mo. I'm sure they have to talk to everybody on the guest list from the fundraiser now that it's being called a murder. I'll handle it. In the meantime why don't you give your

Harley some exercise?" She was wearing her normal black jeans, half boots, and black T-shirt so all she had to do was pick her helmet up from inside the back door and leave.

Oscar walked around the building to the front and heard the car doors open and close while he was working the lock. He turned around when they called out from a few feet away.

"Attorney Oscar Leopold?" The man, whom Oscar assumed was a detective since he was wearing a wrinkled suit and sensible shoes, was in front while his partner, a younger and thinner guy, was a step behind him. There were no patrol cars evident and no guns drawn so it was pretty civilized so far. Oscar heard the Harley start up and take off in the other direction down the alley more quietly than usual.

"Yes, that's me. But the office is closed today."

"I am detective Ramirez and this is detective Hunt, from the Indian River County Sheriff's Department. Do you mind if we come in and ask you a few questions about the political fundraiser two days ago?"

Out of their jurisdiction, Oscar thought immediately. Two counties north. "Oh yes. The murder. I read about it. Terrible. And we were on the grounds just before they say it happened. Come in. But I don't think there's any coffee made yet." He led them through the gallery to his office, gesturing to the two guest chairs as he flipped on the overhead lights.

"Unusual spot for a law office." Detective Ramirez had pulled out a note pad, pen, and small recorder.

"It's strictly part-time. I've tried to quit altogether but the clients won't let me. So I need a place for a sit-down and to sign papers once in a while."

"I think we bumped heads a few years ago when you were with the Public Defender."

"Could be. I handled a lot of cases back then. I hope I wasn't too hard on you. Just doing the job, you know."

"Just like us. Do you mind if I record this?" He turned on the recorder anyway.

"I assume you know your rights, but would you read this card aloud anyway? It's just a formality. We're talking to everybody who was at the party that night."

Oscar read the advice of rights, a tight knot in his stomach. He had been on the other side plenty of times interviewing defendants, and had a minor brush with the system as a defendant himself a year or so back but it was still uncomfortable being the one interviewed. He was being questioned as a potential witness more than as a suspect so he thought it wouldn't take long. But why the Miranda warning? They went over the night's events, including how he happened to be there, whom he talked to, if he saw anyone who seemed out of place or heard anyone say anything that he thought was unusual. Then they wanted to know who Oscar came with.

"The guest list they gave me said you came with a Louise Nevils. Is that right?"

"Yes. And we had a wonderful time for the short while we were there. I feel bad for Sylvia. The candidate? She must be really bummed that this all happened during her event. And the club must be appalled."

"And where can we find Louise Nevils? Do you have her address?"

"No, actually. She had modeled for me—I'm a sculptor in addition to being an attorney, and I always contacted her by telephone."

"You took her on a date and you didn't pick her up and take her home?"

"It wasn't a date. I didn't want to go alone so I asked her to go. Strictly as an escort."

"So she's an escort?" Ramirez looked at Hunt who

smiled slightly.

"No. That's not what I meant. Not a hooker. She just went along for the evening. She wanted to see what the club looked like. A peek at the lifestyles of the rich. She drove here and then drove back home to wherever she lives."

"Can you share her telephone number with us?"

He gave them the number Sydney had provided.

"Do you know a Gerald Prado? Maybe you knew him as Jerry?"

"No. Should I? Was he a guest at the fund raiser?" Oscar cataloged the name since it must be the first victim whose name had not been released to the media.

"How about Earl Santiago?" Both detectives studied Oscar for a reaction.

"The cannibal? Everybody knows about him but I don't think a personal relationship would have been a good idea. I read initially that he accidentally killed himself, doing us all a favor. Now the news says it was some serial killer. What's this about? I didn't know the other one, Charles Atwood, either. I might have talked to him at the party. I talked to several people."

"I was going to get to that. What did you talk about?"

"I imagine just the regular stuff you say when you don't know each other. I probably talked about the club. It was pretty impressive. They have quite a taxidermy collection there. You should check out the men's locker room. The front doors to the place probably cost as much as my car. If I recall Mr. Atwood, he didn't say much other than talk about his golf game. What's going on? Have you got any leads on who this killer is? Do you think it was somebody at the club? You can check with Arnie, the gatekeeper. We left early, thank God."

A few more polite questions and the officers left their cards, gave the standard advice to call if he thought of anything else, then left. Oscar hoped that Atwood actually played golf.

Sydney didn't come home that night and Louise didn't answer her telephone.

2

Sydney read the newspapers and searched the inter-net. According to the *Post*, the killer's victims were likely chosen randomly, since they had nothing in common, not even being in the same age group or city. So the writer said everyone was a potential target. The police claimed no leads and had no suspects. An ongoing investigation they said and asked the public to come forward with information or witnesses.

Having a partner was new to Sydney. She had always worked things out in her head. Alone. That had always been her style. Now she had two heads to work with and Oscar was pretty perceptive. The case was straightforward and didn't require a Sherlock Holmes to figure out the scenario. Since she didn't kill victim one, and only her client knew about her involvement with two and three, the client had to have planted the roses on those two victims. She remembered now the wilted rose behind the Havana Market next to the dumpster. She hadn't seen anything like that at Mo's but then again had no reason to notice such things.

Pastor Luke may have killed the first victim or had someone else do it, so he had to be the one trying to tie them all together. But why? The obvious answer was to take suspicion off of himself for the first murder. He was hiring his own copycat killings and likely was the unnamed source that leaked that information to the press to put pressure on the police to look for a serial killer rather than concentrate on victim one. Pretty clever, but brutal. And how could she prove that without endangering herself and Oscar?

She couldn't just tell the cops about Luke, since he may tell them about her. Irrefutable proof was needed as to the guy who did killing number one. The police would then naturally attribute the next two murders to him.

She spent the night on the beach, thinking about the police at the building. If her cover was blown she had to disappear. She couldn't endanger Oscar and of course didn't want to get caught herself. She had moved on before and could do it again. Money wasn't an issue. The difficulty would be giving up what she had built with Oscar. He was a gentle guy in a lot of ways and resourceful and intelligent in others. He would do what had to be done when it came down to hard choices. And he loved her, in spite of what she did on her night job.

He had learned to accept it once she explained how she got into this and her criteria for taking a job. She tried to bring what she perceived as justice to helpless victims. They appreciated it. Her thanks was measured in dollars. It wasn't unusual to get more than half in the second payment. She liked that, not because of the money so much as it being a thank you for a job done well.

What to do? Was there a solution that would end with the police believing the case had been solved, close the files and remove all suspicion from her? It was possible, but she would have to act quickly. Pastor Luke must be the bad guy. And he was the only one who knew about her involvement so far as she knew. Pastor Luke didn't know who she was and the only contact he had was the website and the offshore bank account which was now closed.

She would shut down the website temporarily. It was registered in one of the old Soviet republics and not subject to U.S. tracing, so that felt safe. But she would shut it down anyway. Then there should be no way anyone could find her.

It had been a mistake to go to the fundraiser, even using a false identity and in disguise. There had been security cameras but she had been careful not to give them a good view of her. Uncharacteristic sloppiness. Taking chances. It wasn't like her to be so overconfident. They could identify Oscar. He hadn't been in disguise. But he had a legitimate reason to be there and the cover story for Louise sounded reasonable, if not provable. Oscar could betray her, of course, but that wouldn't happen. His offer of marriage was genuine, his idea, and might solve the issue of him testifying against her, as unlikely as that seemed right now. But she was careful and this seemed like a reasonable precaution if they could solve the problem of the existing marriage.

Plus—she loved him. So a win-win.

She could kill the Pastor. But that would not end the investigation and in fact might make the cops dig even deeper. He was widely known and well liked and there would be a lot of pressure to find his killer. He didn't fit her criteria for a kill but maybe her own self-preservation would be a new one. Over-thinking a problem wasn't useful. The first instinct was usually the best. She would investigate.

She headed home in the early morning, thinking she should have called Oscar, but didn't want to turn on the burn phone yet, in case the police had the number. They could track her down if she left it on and could get a record of any number she called. She pulled into a shopping center and turned it on briefly to see if there were messages. There was one from Detective Ramirez, asking her to call him back. She would have to think about that. She turned it back off.

Oscar was up, making coffee when she walked upstairs at six-thirty. He kissed her quick with the coffee grinder in hand and tried to pull her close.

"Don't touch me, I stink. I would love a cup of that." She said, pointing at the pot and stepped toward the bathroom, picking up a clean towel from the hall closet on the way. He was still here, so the police presence from yesterday wasn't all that bad.

The morning news was on the small television on the kitchen wall. Oscar was sitting on a bar stool watching while he drank his coffee. It didn't sound like murder news so Sydney poured herself one and sat next to him in her bathrobe.

"If you'd gotten here a half hour earlier we could have saved some water," he said.

She bumped shoulders with him. "Later. We need to debrief. What was with the cops?"

He bumped her back, "Yeah, we need to debrief. You first. What happened with you last night? Where were you?" He turned the sound off on the television and turned his stool toward her. She did the same and their knees touched.

"I thought it best if I stayed away for a while. In case they had the building staked out. No point in making things easy for them. And I had to think. How to get this behind us and what happened to turn this into a serial killer deal."

"Looks like somebody has made you a serial killer surrogate. Not good. But I don't think either of us is under suspicion right now. I'm sure they are interviewing everyone that was at the fundraiser. So the stop here was routine. They have a methodical process that occasionally allows them to solve a case. My being a lawyer will cause them to be very careful before they make any accusations. Or arrests."

"I didn't leave any implicating evidence and they don't know for sure it was someone at the party. There were no interior cameras that I couldn't avoid and those kind of people aren't taking snapshots with their cell phones at an event like that. They had an official photographer, but I just happened to be looking another way whenever she had the camera pointed toward me. Besides, she was pretty busy since the society types were jockeying for position to get their picture in the Sunday society page. People like that don't go to fund-raising parties just to have the chance to write a check."

"How far will they search for Louise?"

"If they get too insistent I'll get back in costume and talk to the cops, red hair and all. Until then we have to find out who's trying to set us up. You must have reached the same conclusion as me."

"Pastor Luke."

"Right. Maybe."

"They spilled a name that I think must be the first victim. Gerald Prado. That will give us a start. We'll see what we can find that the police haven't. Maybe I can come up with some reason why I need to look into things officially. As an attorney. My friend Roy can help me out. With his operation he must have a branch office in Orlando."

"Or I could go in undercover. Check things out as a member of the congregation. Churches always welcome visitors. The victim's mother probably still goes there. I'll see what I can find out from the inside."

"It sounds like we have two workable plans. But first," he undid the tie on her bathrobe and she smiled, "we should have another sort of meeting in the next room."

"An excellent idea."

3

Oscar made the appointment with Roy Early, his former partner, while Sydney finished her preparations to infiltrate the church. Roy and Oscar had gone to law school together in Detroit, then both took the Florida bar exam and went to work in the public defender's office in West Palm before opening their own firm, Leopold and Early. A flip of the coin for whose name was first on the letterhead. They both married, moved into the same subdivision and all seemed well until Oscar's only child died young, leading to his mental collapse and divorce. The firm broke up and Oscar bought the gallery building.

Oscar and Sydney had played key roles in saving Roy from being set up for fraud and murder charges a while back and Roy had recovered nicely. He was grateful to have been cleared and went on to take over a state-wide personal injury firm; spending his time suing insurance companies and making tons of money. Oscar and Roy remained close. Oscar knew he could talk to Roy in confidence about his need to get involved somehow in the affairs of the Gracious Lord Temple, without revealing Sydney's true vocation.

They met that evening on the deck of Roy's forty-four foot trawler, the *Trust Me*, berthed at the North Palm Beach Marina.

"So you need to have a legitimate excuse to poke around the mega-church." Roy twisted the cap off a Kalik, his favorite beer that he brought over by boat from the Bahamas and passed it to Oscar. Oscar knew it was sold in the local grocery store but didn't want to ruin what Roy thought was a special treat by telling him. Roy's red and green Hawaiian shirt was unbuttoned and flanked the sides of his bulging tanned gut. Oscar was wearing his normal uniform these days—khakis and golf shirt.

"I would ideally like to have the ability to use the subpoena power of the courts to do some digging on a possible case I have, as well as help out a friend."

"A close friend I suppose?"

"The closest. Sydney."

"After you called me I looked at our statewide caseload. We actually have two pending cases against the church for injuries sustained from a bus accident. Two kids. I don't know how you're going to justify much investigation beyond the circumstances of the accident, but if you want, I can get you added to the team as of-counsel. My people will be fine with it after I talk to them. I'll tell them you're just going to give it a look but aren't taking it over. Might be some hurt feelings but tough shit. Once they understand you're not in for a share it should be okay. I'll even have Susan in Orlando print up some business cards for you."

"Appreciate it. You might add that I'm investigating another case against the church but haven't decided yet whether to take it. Gives me a little more flexibility." They talked while sitting in the deck chairs and watching the boats cruise by. Facing east there was no sunset to appreciate, but the breeze off the water tempered the heat of the day and Oscar was relaxing for the first time since the mess had started. The boat was big and moved only slightly when a cruiser pushed a big wave at them out from the channel.

They talked of other things and Oscar's mind drifted. Sydney said she would be able to handle the visit to Orlando alone, and Oscar knew she could, but felt he could get access and information unavailable to her. She was on a fishing expedition and he planned on meeting up with her when she finished the church infiltration.

He didn't really want her to try and handle this whole problem by herself. He had a vested interest in solving this serial killer situation. He knew she liked to be in charge and that she was highly capable, but was also quick to violence. He thought he might be able to be the voice of reason under pressure. Or help take out some bad guys himself if need be.

4

To a casual observer, church services at the Gracious Lord Temple were more about drama and entertainment than they were about worship. Their popularity on cable television was mushrooming as much among the curious sectarians as it was the fundamentalist Christians. Everybody wanted to see the snake handling and healing, much like some watched auto races in hopes of seeing a crash.

Sydney checked out the time of the Sunday service online, and by leaving home at six in the morning she was there a few minutes early. The parking lot was already full. She parked in the back and was picked up in a golf-cart-sized open shuttle which transported her and two others to the front doors of the temple. Today's disguise was one of her best.

A quick trip to Target got the white long-sleeved blouse that buttoned up to her neck, as well as a hanging below the knees dark blue skirt, nylons, and black flats. She scrubbed off all makeup, put her hair in a bun, no jewelry, and wore clear eyeglasses with large red plastic frames. She even found a Bible and a black purse to carry. No weapons on this trip except for the knife.

"You're still gorgeous, but I wouldn't recognize you as my Sydney," Oscar said as she left.

There were two greeters at the door. Sydney explained she was newly arrived from Louisville and wanted to see if the church was a good fit for her. Everyone, even the regulars, wore a name tag—the paper kind—and they gave her one, explaining that it made people more comfortable and friendly to know who they were talking to, especially some of the older folks whose memories weren't so good.

Sunday's meeting started with a gathering of the

congregation in the great hall of the Temple. While there were pews in the back, the front half of the room was a large open space where all could assemble. A pulpit, or lectern, or altar—she didn't know what they called it here, was at the front of the room on a two-step-up low stage with curtains at the back. She noted an elevated platform on which a large television camera was mounted, manned by an operator who was tracking the pastor.

Parents brought their children who raced around at will or sat against the wall playing hand-held video games. Pastor Luke walked among all of them with a cordless microphone, his voice amplified over the PA system. Sydney mingled with the crowd, greeting and being greeted via the name tags. Those who knew each other shook hands, even the women, no air kisses.

She was searching for Gerald's mother, Nancy Prado. Her internet search revealed there were only two Prado households, one Nancy Prado and one Clint Prado, each with a household member named Gerald. So it must be mom and dad. Separated or divorced. She was watching for Clint, too, but was hoping to bond with Nancy. The service started with a general call of welcome and introduction of new members and visitors. Many of those in the group brought guitars, banjos, violins, and other instruments so that they could perform solo or join in when others played.

"Welcome everyone," Pastor Luke said into his mike. The sound echoed through the hall. There were five hundred or more people already there and more came in as the service progressed. The elderly or infirm sat in the first rows of pews or in their wheelchairs. Sydney was again surprised at Luke's size. He was well over six feet and his mane of thick blond hair, the dark tan, and the white suit with white tie made him look even more imposing. He looked different than when she saw them at the fundraiser. More in command and actually beaming, perhaps from being so much in his element. His voice was deep and booming.

"I see today we have Brother Wilkes and his family who came all the way from Ocala to be with us here this morning. Praise the Lord." Luke pointed at a man and his wife, who was holding a baby. Brother Wilkes held his hands up and his wife waved her free hand. "And welcome to those I have not yet met. This is your house, the Lord's house, and all are welcome." Not everyone was listening closely to him. Groups were chatting among themselves and children chased each other amongst the adult legs. Several teenagers had moved to the side of the room and were texting or otherwise playing with their devices.

"This morning we are going to show our faith by asking the Lord to bless us with a healing or two. You all know that it says in the good book that you will be healed if your faith is sufficient. I can tell you that the Lord wants to heal you. That if you believe strongly enough in Him you are owed a healing and He will pay that debt. Lord be praised." Luke held his hands up and the room reverberated with Amens.

Luke called those with disabilities to the front of the room. "We are all going to pray for God's children who truly want the power of Jesus to flow through them. Come forward and receive your blessings." Several people worked their way to the front. A grey-haired frail lady, obviously blind, was being helped by a young woman. A man walked forward using an aluminum walker with skids on the legs instead of wheels. Two people in wheelchairs were pushed forward.

Sydney saw that all this was being covered by two roving shoulder-held television cameras and she knew from her research that the service was broadcast live and recorded by cable stations across the country.

Luke latched on to the blind woman.

"Sister, what is your affliction?" He held the microphone to her face.

"I've been blind these many years Brother Anger. I am hoping that with the prayers of all these folks here that I can see again. I don't ask for much. Just a little sight. Even just one eye."

"And Jesus will give you your sight if we all have faith enough." Luke then went to each person who came forward and promised the same thing. Then he made the call to prayer. He squeezed his eyes shut, bowed his head and began praying. So did everyone else. But not the same prayer and not in unison.

"I have a bad leg," someone from the crowd called out.

"Get up here so we can pray for you, brother," Luke called out, waving him forward.

Some went to their knees, praying with clasped hands out loud. Others stood staring upward, also praying loudly. Two women rolled on the floor speaking gibberish quickly, almost without taking a breath, "speaking in tongues" as they said. It was astounding and Sydney didn't know whether to pretend to pray, participate somehow, or just continue to stare. But everyone was so wrapped up in their own method of prayer that she was completely unnoticed. The children ignored the goings-on and continued to play with each other or their electronics, apparently used to all the hubbub.

"I got the power back", said one young man in a long-sleeved white shirt as he talked fast, much like an auctioneer, except his language became incomprehensible. It was cacophony. There was no apparent order to the group prayers. No choreography. Just random acts, speeches, and prayers by individuals.

Sydney was amazed, not having been to many church services since she was a child. Mostly weddings and funerals. None had been like this and she was quite sure this was not the norm. No wonder Luke's television show was so popular. It was more entertainment than any reality show she'd ever seen.

"Don't just sit there and watch, brothers and sisters," Luke said as he gestured to those in the pews. "This is not a performance. Get on your feet. Participate. Feel the spirit and let it lift you up. You at home, get out of that chair, pray, dance, let the Lord know you are with us. We need your prayers." Some began playing instruments and singing. Sydney joined in by dancing with three children while still looking for Nancy's name tag. The whole name tag idea was a good one, she thought. Suppose everyone, everywhere, wore one? Would it be a friendlier, happy world?

The praying died off as a banjo player and guitarist began accompanying a husband and wife singing a hymn, *Water to Wine,* country style in two-part harmony. Others clapped and stomped the floor in time. They were pretty good, Sydney thought. The children continued to stare, and play, and hold onto their parents' legs and run amongst the parishioners. Other musicians joined in.

"The lord's word in the Book of Job says that we cannot trace his hand, but must trust his word. Your faith has not been strong enough. That the Lord did not see fit to heal anyone today is proof and you must redouble your belief from now on."

Then two men came forward carrying a wooden box between them.

"I remind everyone of the word of our Lord in the Gospel of Mark. *'And these signs shall follow them that believe: In my name shall they cast out devils; they shall speak with new tongues. They shall take up serpents; and if they drink any deadly thing, it shall not hurt them; they shall lay hands on the sick, and they shall recover."* He reached into the box and pulled out a four-foot rattlesnake, holding it with one hand halfway along its length. The snake arched back and forth, holding its muscular body horizontal and swaying almost in time to the music that was playing in a corner of the hall.

Luke waved it around, pushing it toward those around him, then took another snake from the box, fondling both. One ran its head down his shirt at the neck and fell to the floor through his shirt sleeve. He picked it up and handed it and another one to others as he removed more from the box. They were passed around, hand-to-hand. The singing continued. People rolled on the floor and kneeled in front of the pews.

Then Pastor Luke pulled out a five-foot timber rattler that promptly bit him on the arm.

Sydney stopped dancing, sure that this was trouble. She had used rattlesnake venom on a job and knew its toxicity. One that size could kill the man unless anti-venom serum was administered immediately. She knew from her research that poisonous snakes killed over a hundred thousand people a year worldwide so this should not be taken lightly. Of course Pastor Luke had God on his side.

"Lord be praised. The serpent has bitten me." Luke handed the snake off to a man who held it in both hands above his head. One camera guy zoomed in on the snake, then panned to Luke and the bleeding wound on his arm. "But I am not afraid. My blessed mother named me after the apostle Luke whose words at Luke 10:19 you all know. *'Behold, I give unto you power to tread on serpents and scorpions, and over all the power of the enemy: and nothing shall by any means hurt you'.* And so, brothers and sisters I am protected."

Luke staggered, then slumped to one knee, but stayed upright. A woman came to him and put her arm under his to steady him. He displayed the blood flowing from the wound to the camera and pulled a handkerchief from his jacket to staunch the flow. "If the good Lord wants to take me now, I am ready to go to the Kingdom."

He stood and held up the bleeding arm. "But now we need to show our faith by giving freely to support the work of Jesus." The assistant pastors moved throughout the crowd with wicker baskets into which cash was deposited by nearly everyone. Sydney was prepared for this and dropped in a twenty. She had located Nancy and stood next to her, waiting for a break in the action so she could make contact.

"I want you all to give," the pastor continued. "Don't say you can't do it. If you can't afford to take care of God and his servants why would God take care of you? Give freely. Those at home who can't be here with us personally can call the number on the screen and we will accept your con-tributions. Every time you smoke one of those cigarettes or look at that expensive big screen television you bought you are taking money away from the Lord's good work. Be honest with Jesus and give what he would think is fair."

One cameraman with a hand-held video camera walked the floor, recording individual scenes, even close-ups on how much was being offered. In the control room Sydney imagined Luke's production manager would cut the scenes together from all the cameras seamlessly for broadcast to the affiliates.

The music played, the snakes were eventually all put back in the box and after a half-hour of more music, talking in tongues, and individual loud praying, the service and the broadcast ended. Luke stumbled back to the area behind the altar, still suffering from the snake bite, his arm having swollen visibly, the choir began to sing a country ballad and gradually the meeting broke up. Sydney hung around, finally talking to Nancy and moved with some others toward the curtain where Luke had exited. She could see him and his retinue. Nancy excused herself and went back to assist Luke. Sydney hung back a bit but followed.

Luke recovered quickly once he was in the office area and out of sight of the congregation.

"What happened with that rattler?" Luke asked Nancy. "My arm is swollen. You want to kill me or what? Do a better job of milking those snakes next time. Find the anti-venom drugs to take care of this for me. Now." He showed his arm, blood still dripping from it.

"I'm so sorry. Let me give you the shot. I was trying to teach some others how to remove the venom. They must not have done a good job," Nancy said.

"This is your responsibility." He stalked off and climbed nearby stairs after getting the injection from her.

Nancy comforted a teenage girl who was crying. "I did my best. I did it the way you showed me," the girl said.

"Don't worry Julie. I can take care of the Pastor. You tried your best."

Nancy headed back to the main room, and Sydney matched her step.

"So you are the snake handler?"

"Yes. I had a bit of nurse's training and am a country girl, not afraid of snakes so I volunteered for the job. It's not so dangerous if you know what you're doing. Of course I'm not like some of them. I wouldn't pick one of those things with my bare hands unless I knew they had been totally devenomed. I use Kevlar gloves when I handle them."

"What do you do with the poison you extract?" Sydney asked.

"I throw it out. The pastor asked me to check on selling it but I found out it's illegal if the snake is a protected species, and most of them are. So down the sink it goes. Shame, because it's valuable."

The television broadcast was over. Back in the main gathering area of the church an announcement was made inviting anyone who could stay to come to the fellowship room for refreshments. Sydney and Nancy shuffled back with the others to a large open low-ceilinged room lit by fluorescents, with no outside windows. A row of tables against one wall held miscellaneous plates of cookies, cakes, and other snacks, apparently brought by the parishioners. A ten-gallon cooler on another table held cold sweet tea and stacks of red plastic cups, the church's contribution.

The crowd went straight for the tables and Sydney thought it would be a good ten minutes before she could get anything should she want it. Nancy held back with her. Sydney held out her hand.

"Hello. I'm Louise. Louise Nevils, as you can see." She grinned and pointed to the name tag.

Nancy shook her hand and gave up a slight smile. "Nancy Prado."

Sydney put her hand to her lips. "Oh. I just realized who you are. I am so very sorry about your son. I cried when I heard about it." She was sincere and put her hand on Nancy's arm, remembering her brother.

"Thank you. Gerald is with the Lord now. I speak to him each night."

"It wasn't clear from the news and I don't want to pry, but how has his father handled it all?"

"I'm separated from Clint." She didn't make eye contact and looked at the floor as she spilled her story quickly. "We had issues and when he drank he became violent. I couldn't deal with it. This has been a nightmare. Now Jerry's been murdered. How can that be? I thank the Lord for the strength I've had just to get up from day to day. I sometimes think Jerry's killer is someone I've seen. The one who caused his death just walking around free. The lord should strike that killer down. I would do it myself if I was sure who he was and could muster the courage."

"Does Clint live around here?"

"A few miles from here. Jerry stayed overnight with him sometimes. I offered alternate weekends. I think Jerry enjoyed getting away from me. Moms and teenage boys don't always get along. Of course Jerry, bless him, had trouble getting along with everyone except the pastor. Thanks to Pastor Luke I got this job here at the church after Jerry's death. I thought I might know more about what motivated Jerry and see the kind of people he may have associated with. They have been kind, almost a second family. The job's volunteer but keeps me busy and I can be near the pastor. I want to get to know him better." She looked up again, a trace of a smile.

"What about Jerry? Is there anything you suspect that the police aren't looking into? Things that you think might have happened or people you think were involved?"

"No. The sheriff has been very nice. And Pastor Luke has gone out of his way to help me. He and Jerry were very close, you know. I told the sheriff all I knew. This was a terrible shock. I know teenage boys are into a lot of experimentation, so maybe he met someone on the internet like Pastor Luke said. I don't really know. I just wish I could wake up to this being a horrible dream. I am trying very hard to believe Jerry's death will be avenged."

She was silent for a moment, the anger gradually softening in her face. "How about you? I haven't seen you here before, how did you happen to come here today?"

Sydney, who was in the revenge business, realized she was on an unpaid mission to do just what Nancy wanted.

"I'm moving here from Louisville. I've been watching the meetings on television and thought it would be quite an experience to see everything in person."

"Was it?"

"Absolutely. It was very powerful. I may just join the church but I want to come a few more times to be sure." They were still standing aside and the crowd at the food table didn't seem to be thinning. Not that Sydney had much interest in the offerings, but she was going with whatever would keep her next to Nancy.

"Would you like to go out for some brunch away from here?" Sydney asked. "My treat. I'm new and don't know my way around. It would be a great help if I could pick your brain. Find out the best place to get an apartment and shop and stuff."

"Yes. I would like that. I haven't done anything since Jerry..." she looked around, as if looking for someone, then turned back to Sydney. "There's a restaurant in a little strip mall not too far from here. Clint and I used to go there. You could follow me."

Chico's should have been a Mexican restaurant if its name meant anything, but it was all-American. Not a diner, more of a dinner restaurant that had a lunch menu. There were even white tablecloths, but it wasn't expensive. They were the only customers so far, which was usually a warning sign to Sydney, but she wasn't there for the food.

"This is all new to me," Sydney said as they sipped their tea and waited for their orders. "This thing about healing. Are you into this? I mean, have you ever seen Pastor Luke heal anyone?"

"Actually, I don't believe the pastor is capable of

healing anyone. But I have seen people healed. There was a man who had an inoperable cancer behind his right eye, going into his brain. The doctors said there was nothing they could do. He came to the church and we had several prayer meetings where everyone concentrated and prayed for him to be healed."

"And?'

"And the tumor gradually went away. Six months later they couldn't find it. It could have been a coincidence. But what I think is that his body healed itself. Have you ever heard of the placebo effect?"

"Yeah. That's where someone thinks they are going to be cured by taking a drug and their body responds by curing them, even when it turns out the drug was fake." The waiter brought their food and they stopped talking until he left.

"Exactly. That's what believing is all about. When Pastor Luke says we can be cured if only we believe hard enough it's not just a bunch of religious magic he's talking about. A strong belief can actually cause miracles."

"I guess I agree up to a point. Raising the dead and walking on water might be pushing the limit though. Interesting."

After Sydney covered her tracks by asking about the best areas to live and got recommendations on shopping and dining, she turned the conversation again to Nancy's son, Gerald.

"Have you been able to talk to Jerry's father about the death?"

"No. Clint wouldn't answer his phone or my texts. I stopped by the house. His van was there but he wouldn't answer the door. I'm starting to worry. He's probably upset. I told you he was a paraplegic didn't I? Maybe I should call the police to see if they can check on him."

"I didn't know. Was he in the service?"

"Afghanistan. Lost both legs and couldn't get the prosthesis to work for him. He has to use the wheelchair and it has been hard on him. I took Jerry away because of his drinking and drugs and the violence. But he was acting better so lately I've been letting Jerry see him. I mean I was, until…"

"Do you suspect anyone for Jerry's death? I mean, was there anyone whom he saw regularly who might have been involved?"

"He was victimized and died. That much I know. They say serial killer but I don't know about all that. I enrolled him in the church school here so he would be safe. The pastor counseled him and assured me that Jerry was working through his troubles. He advised me not to get a psychiatrist involved; that he could guide him. He promised. Now look what's happened." Nancy used the napkin to dab her eyes and blow her nose.

"What troubles did he have that might have required a psychiatrist?"

"His school work was sliding. He skipped school a lot and hung out at the mall. His computer was password protected and he wouldn't let me see it. I took it away once, but he needed it for school. I don't know what he was mixed up in but he changed. He was distant. Maybe it was drugs or the wrong people he was seeing. At that age kids are trying to break away from their parents. The pastor was in over his head trying to help him. Jerry needed a professional. I shouldn't have listened. I can't help but think that he shares the blame. Lord forgive me."

"Have you seen a lawyer?"

"I thought about it but don't know what they can do. Jerry's dead."

"Sometimes they can make people account for what

they did so it wouldn't happen to any other kids in the future. I would be happy to help you find one you can trust. I used to be a legal secretary. Here's a card of someone I know you can trust. Just to get information. See what your rights are." Sydney fished from her purse one of Oscar's cards and handed it to Nancy.

"Okay. I guess it wouldn't hurt. Something has to be done to make this right."

The card was still on the table when they left.

5

Luke was home by eleven the night of the fund raiser for Judge Pocholi. The fact of Charles "Mo" Atwood's death didn't bother him. Atwood was an evil man who deserved what he got. That was why Luke had chosen him as a victim. With Luke's political connections it wasn't difficult to get invited to the fundraiser, even though he had never met the judge. Those in his political party stuck together, supporting each other's candidates. Especially those with deep pockets.

But who was the killer? There was no way of knowing what the Pest Control person looked like. He had to have been one of the guests. Or did he? Maybe it was an ambush by someone who snuck in. Or someone posing as one of the help. He had people in authority who could ask around. If some stranger was at the fund raiser they would know. It was too hard to get into the complex to imagine someone just walked in and took Mo out.

But maybe that's how it was done. Luke was certainly no expert in killing. He had asked for forgiveness from God; privately of course, and was confident he would be forgiven for Jerry's death. He didn't think he needed forgiveness for Earl Santiago or Mo Atwood who were both surely burning in hell.

Despite the thirty-year difference in their ages Luke and Jerry had what Luke considered a unique and special love. Jerry had been an eager student in Luke's Sunday school class; always asking questions and anxious to do well in the one-on-one faith meetings. They had been naked in Jerry's room when it happened, rolling around on the bed just having fun, he thought. Now Jerry's death threatened to destroy Luke as well. He simply could not let that happen. The sex game was Jerry's idea and he said he had done it before. So why, Luke thought, should anyone else have to suffer because of his screw-up?

It all started as Jerry's experiment, with Luke's help, to step as close as possible to the thin line between life and death to increase the pleasure of orgasm without dying. From his look and actions Luke thought Jerry had the experience he desired. But he never woke up to tell. The trace of a smile on the lifeless face had seemed obscene. Pastor Luke had gently closed Jerry's eyes and wiped the trickle of blood that ran from his right ear. It was Jerry's fifteenth and last birthday, symbolic since Luke had first met Jerry on his twelfth.

He looked it up later on the library computer. Auto-erotic asphyxiation. The dictionary said it was usually associated with masturbation. A sin in itself. Sexual things should be shared with others. Giving pleasure rather than taking it was the right way, but that only worked if both parties shared the same belief. This was how it was supposed to work: a guy or his partner in this case, would tie a rope or belt around the neck, then tighten it, exerting pressure on the carotid arteries on each side of the neck, cutting off blood flow to the brain temporarily to theoretically increase the pleasure at orgasm. If alone, a person would sit on the floor, leaning against a door. The belt would then be tied to a door knob and the weight of the person's body when he slid slowly down would supply the pressure.

It wasn't the same as choking. The air supply wasn't cut off, just the blood flow. So unconsciousness could happen in seconds and you had to be careful since brain death could occur in less than five minutes. It was a knockout hold sometimes used by the police to subdue a perp. The police were trained to know when to let the pressure off. It was also getting to be popular as a quick and easy method of suicide. Much more pleasant and less visually disturbing than hanging oneself from a tree limb. Luke knew now he should have known more before trying Jerry's dangerous game. After a desperate attempt at CPR failed he wiped down everything that could show fingerprints.

No one would have accepted it as an accident. It would be on everyone's lips. If they found out that Luke and Jerry had been intimately involved over the past two years they would naturally assume Luke was the guilty one. The former football player-pervert-pastor preying on slender helpless young men. They wouldn't understand the love that Luke had for his boys. So he had been forced to cover it up.

They had used Jerry's bathrobe belt for the game. It was green velour and felt nice on the skin. Luke wrapped it around Jerry's neck as instructed and twisted, tightening more and more during the sex act. He thrashed and moaned, but Jerry had said to keep up the pressure on the belt no matter what, but to release it at just the right moment.

The right thing would have been to cover him, give him some small bit of respect. Shield his private parts with the sheet. But then it wouldn't look like an accident, so he had stopped himself. He had gone to his knees at the bedside and recited the Lord's Prayer with his head bowed and eyes gripped closed. He then placed a small bible and a white rose in a small vase he had brought from the church on the window sill. Jerry had gone to the Lord, a better place, so there had been no need to cry. Luke slipped out of the house into the garage where he had hidden his car and went back to the church, vainly wishing that it had never happened and praying that his involvement would not be discovered or suspected.

The next day the news of Jerry's supposed suicide had reached Luke through Mary, his wife, while he was getting coffee in the employee lounge at the Gracious Lord Temple. Luke was the head Pastor and founder of the church but had an administrative staff who dealt with fundraising, office work, and production of his live Sunday morning radio and television show. All told there were a dozen or so people in the offices that day. Several were in the lounge.

He set his coffee cup down and clasped his hands to his chest. "Lord help us. That poor child."

Mary touched his arm, tears working down her cheeks.

"I need to meet with Jerry's mother, Nancy, to console her. See what we can do as a family to ease her suffering," Luke said.

Mary sniffled, found a paper napkin on the coffee serving table and dabbed her eyes. "Actually, brother Anger, she's here. In the waiting room and has asked to see you."

Luke went to his upstairs office and Mary led Nancy in. Luke came around his desk, hugged her, kissed her on the lips as was his custom with men and women, and motioned to the couch. Her face was reddened but she was not crying. She held her purse on her lap with both hands.

"It's the Lord's will. Gerald is looking down on us now. He's at the foot of our father," she said.

"Glory to God. Praise Jesus." Luke sat next to her and took her hand.

"And how is Clint taking the loss? I can't imagine he would be able to deal with the loss of his son very well in his condition."

"I called. He won't see me. I was hoping you might reach out to him."

"I will do what I can in this trying time. I have always hoped the two of you would work out your troubles and get back together. We offer couples counseling."

"Clint is angry and sad at the same time. And I can't go back with him. His disability and trouble with the law is more than I can handle. Maybe if he hadn't gotten hurt in the war things would have been different." She opened her purse for another tissue.

"Mysterious ways, mysterious ways. But it's time to speak of worldly things, Sister Prado. You are going to have to deal with the news people now. Ignoring the press only lets them come to their own conclusions. I would like you to refer anyone who tries to interview you to contact me here at the Temple. Those reporters can twist things around and make situations seem worse than they really are. We can speak for you and will do whatever else we can to help. And I want to plan a special prayer service for your son. You can have it here without charge. I know everyone will want to pray for you and Gerald."

"Praise the Lord, Brother Anger, and thank you. But not without charge. I want to make a free-will offering in Jerry's name. Don't say no. This is right. And what would have been his inheritance I am leaving to the Temple to promote your good works."

"Thank you Jesus." Luke had raised his hands and eyes to the ceiling then looked back at her. "You will get your reward in Heaven for the good you do on earth, Sister."

Who could imagine the Jerry would have died so easily? Accidental death is what Luke considered it. It was certainly not intentional. The problem was that the local sheriff hadn't stuck with the accidental suicide theory as Luke had hoped. After an autopsy they said that Jerry could not have self-inflicted the bruises on his neck and that someone else had to have been involved.

God had forgiven him, Luke was sure of that. And while Luke had paid the killer for Earl's and Mo's death with the church offerings, he didn't actually do the physical act of killing them, so his hands were clean. It was some other evil person who did that sort of thing for a living. The killer would get his punishment of eternal damnation one day as well as the two who had been killed. It was in the scriptures and if there was one thing Luke was sure of, it was the literal truth of the Bible.

"*Eye for eye, tooth for tooth, hand for hand, foot for foot,* Exodus 21:24," he muttered.

Luke confessed to Mary shortly after Jerry's death. She was angry but moved quickly to provide damage control. The idea to make it look like a serial killing was hers, and she came up with the idea to find a hit man and put roses and bibles at the other two murder scenes. In the initial investigation of Jerry's death no one had noticed the rose and bible in Jerry's room and Nancy had removed them when she cleaned. Luke knew only what he saw in books and films about serial killers, but read that sometimes they left a signature, a marker of some kind. The rose and bible, though not intended as such a thing with Jerry, seemed to Mary to be made to order.

The objects had initially been overlooked and not considered significant. They were only discovered after Luke's tip and after the police reviewed the available crime scene photos. Nancy had kept the glass vase and bible, but the rose was gone and the vase had been washed. The police sent the bible in for forensics, but it appeared to be new and had no usable prints other than Nancy's.

Luke made the call linking the three murders just as he and Mary had planned. He had driven sixty miles to Bartow and with a handful of quarters used a rare pay phone to call the *Palm Beach Post*. He left a message with a receptionist with the names of the three victims, and suggested she have someone call the police and ask if they had found a white rose and a pocket-sized Bible at each crime scene.

They had hoped to make it look like a serial killer and the plan worked. The pressure was now off Luke and they hoped the investigation into Jerry's death would take a different tack.

Luke continued his work. Running his many-legged Church operation was like being the CEO of a mid-sized corporation. There were meetings with accountants, personnel issues, scheduling speaking engagements, his regular youth counseling, preparing for weddings, the list never seemed to end.

Luke came to this form of ministry naturally. He grew up in the hills of Kentucky as one of six children of a coal mining family. They were Pentecostals and their church was a non-denominational loosely knit group that met as much for social reasons as religion.

There just wasn't anything else to do other than church related activities in the poor area where they lived. The head pastor was a miner himself and had no formal religious training, nor was he ordained by any established church. He was the prayer leader more than anything else. Their core value was that the Bible was literally true. Every word of it. They conveniently ignored such things as logic, science, and history, believing devoutly that if there was some issue interpreting the Biblical language, or if there seemed to be contradictions and inconsistencies, this was the fault of the inability of man to understand the intent of God.

Two days after Luke's telephone call to the *Post* he was called by the Indian River County Sheriff's department ninety miles southeast of Orlando. They asked him to come in and talk about Jerry's death since he knew Jerry, his friends, and the family. Pastor Luke was well known in Florida and that celebrity allowed him to require the detectives to come to him. The appointment was the next day. They said it was routine, trying to find a link between the three deaths.

The local police had given up questioning the townspeople and checking Jerry's friends, having bought into the State Police and FBI theory that this was a serial killer they were after. The new officers from Indian River County covered the same ground with their questions and had uncovered nothing new. Luke's interview with the detective was perfunctory. They had no reason to suspect him and were very polite as they took notes while talking to him with Mary present. Neither of them volunteered any information he didn't already know.

Pastor Luke now felt comfortable getting back to business. He promised himself he would be more careful in the future in his intimate counseling with his flock. Experience had shown and he knew himself that promises were easy to make to oneself but just as easily forgotten.

One day Julie Weston stopped him in the hallway outside the recording studio. It was after six and the employees had gone home.

"Pastor Anger? Could we talk for a minute?"

She was wearing her school uniform. A below-the-knees plaid dress and white short-sleeve blouse. It had been Luke's idea to have the student uniforms. He thought it would avoid the prideful displays of clothing and put all the students on equal footing. Mary and some of the others were also watchful that the outlandish dress styles teens wore in town would not infiltrate their charter school. Her shoulder-length blond hair was held back with a headband that matched the skirt.

"What is it, Julie?"

"It's about the scholarship. You know—the one I applied for through the Temple program? I thought with my work on the mission I had a good chance. I wondered if my application was complete or if there was anything else I can do to increase my chances. I haven't heard anything and you sort of promised."

Luke hesitated for only a few seconds. She was referring to one of the scholarships the Temple awarded every year to deserving students. They were based on merit and by the time they graduated from high school some students had accumulated several. Julie had plenty of merit in Luke's view. "I'll have to check the file. Why don't you come up to my office and we'll see where it stands. We'll take the elevator."

Julie had been one of his favorites since he and Mary started counseling her at fourteen. Now at fifteen she was in her freshman year at the local charter school the Temple had founded. Luke would be sorry to see her graduate and wanted to enjoy her company as much as possible before she left. He'd had a few intimate encounters with her, but these had cooled after her trip to Mexico with Mary on missionary work. He felt they had a special relationship that went beyond mentor and disciple but she had lately preferred to counsel with Mary rather than him, though he did help her from time to time and came to him before she would confide anything to her parents.

"I haven't had the chance to ask you before, but how did you enjoy the mission work with Sister Anger?" The so-called mission was actually a condo on the beach in Costa Rica funded by the church, but visitors were required to spend a few hours volunteering at a local orphanage to make it look legitimate.

"It was fabulous. We did good work there. I can't wait for another chance like that. To do mission work, I mean."

"You are a wonderful asset to the church and to Mrs.

Anger and me. Remember the word of the Lord in Genesis 2:18: '*It is not good that the man should be alone; I will make him a helpmate.*' That is you and Mary, Julie. Helpmates. God's word."

They exited into Luke's office. He had no files up there and Julie didn't ask about that omission. She barely resisted when he pulled her to him and they were both quickly naked and on the couch.

They had been in the office for about fifteen minutes, just getting started really, when the worst possible thing happened.

Mary came into the Temple. Luke heard her talking downstairs and was shocked since she was supposed to be visiting her mother in the nursing home. He jumped to his feet and peeked out the window that looked down into the auditorium below. She was with two other women and they were headed to the stairs that led to the office.

"Hurry, hurry, hurry, Julie! Get dressed. Go to the elevator. We don't want to ruin your chances for the scholarship. Mrs. Anger is on her way up." Luke pulled on his pants and searched for the rest of his clothes, dressing quickly.

"Why can't we just tell her? Or let her find us. Then we can be together all the time like you just said you wanted." Julie made no move to get up, and was still sprawled lewdly on the couch in an unexplainable state of undress.

"Move! Now!" Luke whispered loudly, but not so loud those downstairs would hear. He found his shoes and was happy he had worn the slip-ons with no laces.

She glared at him, then grabbed at her clothing and shoes and stalked naked to the elevator. Despite the situation and her apparent anger, Luke admired the view as she walked away.

Mary came in, greeting Luke and introducing her friends who were new to the church, potential donors to the building fund, who wanted some face time with the famous Pastor. They stayed only a few minutes. When they were leaving, Mary stuck her head back in.

"Luke, I kicked your pink panties under the couch. This is once too many, but at least it's not a boy this time. I think you know what this is going to cost you."

"I will do as I please. Just as you do. I don't need to be berated. I've done enough for you as it is," he said, though she had already walked out and he knew he would accede to her demands. Mary would now have more leverage. He had already turned over many of their joint assets to her name alone to keep her quiet. That was her way of evening the score. Leaving him would be a financial disaster for both of them at this point. She knew that so she just put more toys on her side of the playground. He had his own rewards, but they were intangible memories of quick dalliances that had to be followed up with even more experiences to keep them real. The risk was high, but so far Mary and the boys and girls involved were the only ones aware of his obsession. They were all compensated and none complained. Luke and Mary still maintained a boisterous and frequent sexual life so it wasn't as if he were needy. His obsession was a sickness apart from sex, a driving thirst for youth that could never be slaked.

He knew that leaving the panties had not been an accident. Julie was getting a dangerous fixation on him and misunderstood their relationship. He had done too much for her. It happened from time-to-time. He decided to slow things down, to give her the scholarship with the unspoken message that it could be retracted. In another couple of years she would be off to college seducing boys her own age. She would have no evidence of their relationship should she decide to come forward. He made sure he always used condoms and had never been caught alone with her. This had been too close a call. He promised himself to be more cautious in the future. He would stop. That would be best.

Mary was a continuing annoyance, but had been manageable up until now. If she would just leave him alone. Mind her business. He gave her everything anyone could want but it was never enough. She thought she could do without him, that she could run the church. But he still had the celebrity and was the rainmaker, not her. She had tried to perform the service once when he took sick but it hadn't gone well. She just didn't have the showman spirit in her. So she knew she had no choice but to indulge him for now.

He imagined that at some point she might decide she had enough money of her own to no longer need him. When the day came that she thought she had enough of an upper hand to ruin him, he knew how to solve that problem as well.

People died all the time. Why not her?

6

Oscar was buying all the newspapers he could find, including the *Palm Beach Post*, the *Miami Herald, Florida Today*, the *New York Times* and the *Orlando Sentinel*. He went through them page by page in his office. The recycling bin he had brought inside and placed next to his desk was nearly full. A daily search on the internet supplemented his information gathering, but hadn't revealed anything more than a lot of blog opinions on what was happening.

"There's no new news on the serial killer," he said to Sydney. "The reporters do their best to make a story of it but they just rehash what's already been said and interview so-called experts on serial killers to fill space."

"Yeah, you can't help but think that they can hardly wait for a new body to be discovered. They will be real disappointed if the killings stop. Maybe I should issue press releases." She was standing in his doorway rubbing a cold beer on her forehead. "Is the air conditioning going to be fixed any time soon?"

"The guy says he'll be here today."

"This is Florida. Like the Caribbean. Today means today only if the fish aren't biting or something else doesn't come up, like happy hour. Anyway, if there isn't another killing soon, interest in the story will fade. Something new will come along. Politicians who can't keep it in their pants can always be relied on for the next scandal."

"Ain't that the truth? But that's not going to stop the task force. The only thing I found was this little item from the Orlando paper. Some details came out about the Orlando killing. The sexual aspect is pretty seductive to the public. They get used to the sensationalism so the more lurid and appalling the more it becomes appealing. They blow things way out of their importance especially on the cable shows like Nancy Grace, who's beginning her own campaign to bring the serial killer to justice. Fortunately for those of us who don't want more publicity the serial murders aren't the main focus of her show since she's been concentrating for three weeks on another Florida child kidnapping. Why do all the weird things happen in Florida?"

"I don't think you can blow this out of proportion. It is, you have to admit, a pretty big story. There hasn't been a good serial killing case on the news in this part of the country in almost a year," Sydney said.

"You would think that would be approaching a record, but they say there are between fifty to two hundred serial killers operating in this country at any point in time, depending on who you ask and how they define the term. But this isn't really a serial killing. It's us and Luke and whoever else. You might call it multiple murders, but not serial killing."

"The truth is even more bizarre than what they know. And I hope they never know the truth."

Sydney had stopped taking on any new clients temporarily—maybe permanently—she offered to Oscar. He hoped so but didn't press. If they could skate clear of the existing mess he was ready to spend all of his time running the gallery, sculpting, with just a tiny bit of law. It wasn't a bad life. Sydney had gotten very involved in the bonsai project. There was a local bonsai society that she had joined and went to a weekly meeting. Oscar had been invited but declined, knowing she was just being polite by making the invitation but also knowing that she wanted the bonsai thing to be hers, not theirs.

The shelving on the balcony had increased to

accommodate her collection, but there was still room to sit, and Oscar kind of enjoyed having his morning coffee and evening glass of wine amongst the tropical plants. He, and he hoped she, was considering marriage and they were turning into quite the domestic couple if you ignored the conspiracy to murder they shared.

After much cajoling, Sydney agreed to Oscar's request to try and get a concealed weapons carry permit. He already had one and reminded her of the time he had been charged with a felony for failing to have the necessary permissions after an altercation in a parking lot with some very bad characters. He shot one, not killing him, and in the end the case had been dismissed, but he had learned his lesson and got the license. Sydney was wary of the federal background check but wouldn't mind having the permit since she was nearly always armed anyway.

Of greatest concern was the fingerprint requirement, not the background check. Her background under the Louise Nevils' name was clear, so there would be no arrests or mental issue on record. The fingerprint thing was different. There was no way she would voluntarily put her fingerprints into the system. The application for the permit had to have a fingerprint card attached, or a computer scan of her prints, but she thought she might have a way around that. A local pawn shop had a gun range on site and since guns were one of the top things pawned, they also offered classes to qualify for the carry permit. She could get the application and fingerprint card from them and take the class there, or better yet at a gun show.

Sydney's only female acquaintance was her hairdresser, Gloria, who was cash-short but had never been in any legal trouble. They talked, Sydney explained, and in the end she was eager to take a thousand dollars to go to the local sheriff's office and get the fingerprint card needed for the permit application. Sydney explained that she needed the prints but couldn't use her own because of an issue in the past and that she would replace Gloria's name and address with her own once the card was in hand. No risk to Gloria, she assured her.

She assured Gloria she needed the carry permit to protect herself, which seemed believable to Gloria given the loose state of law and order in West Palm. She handed the card over to Sydney who took it back to her office computer and made a facsimile with Gloria's prints, Sydney's picture, and Louise Nevils' information. The only way there could be a problem would be if Gloria committed some crime and left her prints behind and she then implicated Sydney. Unlikely, Sydney thought.

Oscar was busy but he agreed to accompany her on a gun-buying expedition. She had disposed of several in her cache and was re-arming. The annoying need for background checks, three-day cooling-off periods, and federal registrations could be easily avoided for those who knew how to game the system.

Oscar was an attorney but had never bothered to look into the gun laws in detail until he got his own carry permit. Even so, Sydney had a few things to show him about the holes in the firearms sales laws.

"So here's the deal. Let's say I can't legally buy a handgun. Maybe I'm a convicted felon, or a non-citizen or have been in a mental institution. But I want a gun. What do I do?" she asked.

"I've heard that going to a gun show is the way to go. There're a good percentage of felons who try to buy a gun and submit to the background check but it doesn't catch them so they buy a gun for cash and it's a done deal." Oscar was in his studio hollowing a sculpture preparatory to drying and firing it.

Sydney sat on the modeling stool, for the first time sitting there fully dressed.

"Yeah. That works sometimes. The system isn't perfect. But what if it doesn't fail and they deny the purchase? The guy is now on police radar and they know that he tried to buy a gun. Could be a parole violation. Dangerous. No. What he does is buy a gun from a private seller. Florida, and a bunch of other states, doesn't require a background check when it's a private person-to-person sale. And there's no registration requirement here so no one knows the transaction even took place."

"How do you find someone who wants to sell a gun? Ask around at your local biker bar?"

"You could. Or you could go to a gun show. People will sometimes be selling out of their trunks in the parking lot. If you don't want to wait for the next show just go online. There are a half-dozen websites where anyone can list a gun for sale with pictures and everything. Kind of like Ebay for firearms." She jumped off the stool and tried to smooth some of the clay on the figure he was working on.

"Don't touch. That sounds illegal, but knowing the conservative state of the legislature in the south I'm not surprised. Have you found one online you want?"

"Yes. I emailed the seller and he wants to meet. But not at his home, at the county boat ramp parking lot on the Intracoastal. People get a little paranoid when it comes to things like this. So I thought it would be good to have you along for backup in case he tries something silly. All you have to do is lean against the car where he can see you while I look at the merchandise."

They made the buy. Oscar watched while Sydney checked the gun over. It looked like a small Glock nine-millimeter. She pulled the slide back, looked inside the action, put the empty clip in and popped it out, seemed satisfied and the seller put it in a paper bag for her while she handed him a roll of bills. Nothing unusual happened. It was as if she was buying a used fishing reel. Oscar thought he should write a complaining letter to the editor, but remembered that he and Sydney benefitted from this loophole considering the business they were now both in.

Getting the actual carry permit turned out to be even easier than she had imagined. There seemed to be a gun show every weekend in South Florida. This one was at the county fairgrounds and advertised a two-hour express concealed weapon permit class for forty-five dollars. The admission to the show itself was collected at a table sponsored by the National Rifle Association; though they made it clear they were not sponsoring the gun permit classes.

Inside were over two hundred tables of exhibitors. Nearly any small weapon was available for sale. There were Samurai swords, knives of all kinds, stun guns, pepper spray canisters in designer colors and of course firearms. These ran the full gamut from handguns so small they would fit in the palm of your hand unnoticed to large bore assault rifles with high capacity magazines, laser sights, and built-in tripods. Revolvers, semi-automatics, antique guns, shotguns, pistols that could fire shotgun shells. It was an amazing display of firepower and there were hundreds of people jostling to get close to the tables.

The class was at the back of the building in a room that held approximately one hundred folding chairs in rows facing a whiteboard. But first she had to go through the registration line, then the photo line for the passport sized photo required for the license before the class actually began. She was surprised that about forty percent of her classmates were women. The rest were mostly white men and Latinos with only one African-

American signed up.

In two hours she learned nothing new, except the situations where it was okay to kill somebody under the Stand Your Ground law, and what to say to the police after you did it. The instructor explained that the right answer was that you shot the victim because "I believed I was in imminent danger of my life and I had to shoot to protect myself". They advised to say the same thing on a 911 call and to be sure to be the first one to call 911 so your message would be recorded before a neighbor called in claiming you shot someone in cold blood. Informative and everyone listened closely.

Then the group leader went through the application line-by-line so that everyone filled it out correctly. Another half-hour waiting for the notary stamp and she was done. They were then sent to a local pawn shop that had a gun range. This was to show they had training in the use of firearms safety. Sydney used their gun, a western style Smith & Wesson revolver, snapped off five quick shots, all in a one inch group on the target and that was that. In ninety days, they said, Louise Nevils would get her concealed weapons permit in the mail. Not only that, there was reciprocity amongst states with similar laws so she could carry her weapons legally throughout most of the southern and western states and much of the Midwest.

This was a very handy piece of paper for someone in Sydney's business.

7

The opening of the art show at the Rose Madder Gallery was uneventful at first. People dribbled in two, four, and six at a time. Since it was a national show only eight of the twenty exhibiting artists appeared for the opening. The usual group from the neighborhood headed to the free wine and cheese, not looking at the paintings.

The opening was advertised as being from six to eight o'clock. By seven there were fifty people or so in the gallery or outside on the sidewalk talking. Sydney helped by supervising the caterer and making sure none of the neighborhood kids snuck a drink.

It was all going well until Judge Pocholi arrived with her crew.

"Oscar! You came to my function and were so generous I thought I'd bring some people and return the favor. We're on our way to dinner so we can only take a quick peek." She hugged him, even gave him a cheek-to-cheek, and continued to hold his arm after he pulled loose. She was wearing the basic black dress and heels that complemented her tall thin figure. A different look than Oscar had ever seen on her in court.

"Thanks Sylvia. Can I get you a glass of wine?"

"Oh, no. I know you're busy talking to everyone. Believe me I know it's a chore. We need to get together when things settle down. How do the kids say it? Hang out? I can't stay. Let me look around and I'll move on." She was using the event as a campaign stop. Her retinue all had buttons pinned on starring her picture and reading *Pocholi for Judge*. He wouldn't have been surprised if they started passing them out. Then she went to the refreshment table.

Sydney was there, standing nearby, playing hostess, and talking to one of the artists, though she had Sylvia on her radar when interrupted.

"Haven't we met? Sylvia Pocholi. Weren't you at my party?" She held out her hand.

Sydney hesitated. They had indeed met but that was when she was the green eyed, Auburn haired Louise, the one with the tattoo, not the leather-skirted, black-booted, body-stockinged, raven-haired one with brown eyes and black eye-shadow. She took Sylvia's hand.

"I don't believe so. Sydney Simone. Sorry I missed your fundraiser. I heard about it, but I was tied up. Nice to meet you." Sydney now pulled Sylvia gently past her by the hand before she could say anything else, a little payback, and moved on to talk to someone else. That was, she hoped, good enough. Sylvia had recognized her but didn't make the connection to Oscar. Or maybe she was just guessing that Oscar would have brought a date even if she didn't remember who it was. It could be a fatal error if the memory came back. But Sydney didn't like the conversation. Little mistakes add up. She could be in jeopardy.

8

Central Florida, away from Orlando and a handful of oasis cities scattered inland, is primarily rural and the people are for the most part the conservative red state sort. For a good share of the people the church is the social center of their community with nearly all activities tied in one way or another to it. Your friends are fellow church-goers and you share the same political and moral beliefs.

There is another element in the populace that doesn't get much press but is very much a force. The so-called Florida rednecks. The less educated, alligator-hunting, beer-drinking, trailer-living, manual-labor types that have their own agendas, and their own activities.

They are disdainful of the snow-bird Yankees who they blame for their unemployment and ruining the economy of the state by overbuilding and driving up the cost of housing and everything else. At least that was the way Luke saw the state of the state. Years ago he would have been called a redneck himself, a Florida cracker; even though he was from Kentucky, had he not bettered himself with education and the call to the church.

His father moved south to work with Luke's uncle when Luke was a boy. Luke's uncle was a coastal fisherman working with nets from small boats for the inshore species. When his uncle Matt was born the barrier islands were mostly unpopulated and used primarily to graze cattle and grow citrus. There were bountiful catches of fish back then and no rules against gill netting, harvest limits, or closed seasons. Expensive commercial fishing licenses were not heard of and whatever a man could catch and sell was his. Sebastian was on the mainland overlooking a mile-wide swatch of the Atlantic Intracoastal Waterway.

The waterway is saltwater, like a river skirting the coastline, separating the barrier islands from the mainland. It is sometimes no wider than a canal and in other places nearly a mile wide, occasionally winding out into the Atlantic. It stretches from Massachusetts to Texas, providing a navigable route around the entire east and southern coasts of the country for commercial and recreational boating. Kept open by the Army Corps of Engineers' continual dredging, it was one of the early federal programs that particularly benefitted and even created some of the coastal villages of Florida.

Things had changed, as they do. Now the oceanfront barrier islands were shoulder-to-shoulder with hotels, condo-towers, and mini-mansions, and the coastal communities had been taken over on the I-95 corridor by people from New York and New Jersey. On the Gulf Coast along I-75 those from Ohio, Ontario, and Michigan slid down to nest for the winter. The pre-1960 locals had been overrun, outvoted, bought out, and moved inland or to the poor areas of the big cities. Orlando was just a small town back then with big ideas to come. Certain types knew how to capitalize on change.

Luke's father was not one of them, and died bitter and poor, leaving Luke to survive by way of the church. After securing a scholarship and working any job he could get for tuition, he finally graduated from Baylor University in Waco, Texas. It was originally a Baptist college and suited to his chosen profession. He went home and opened his own ministry in an empty storefront near Orlando, just after the city was engulfed by the Disney/Universal Studios sprawl. Good timing on his part. He was on the crest of a huge influx of potential parishioners and made the most of it.

Radio was an ideal way to spread his message and his

carnival-barker preaching style and the unorthodox nature of the service itself made the sermons lively entertainment. Had he not gone into preaching he would have done well as an infomercial spokesman offering to double your order if you called in the next fifteen minutes. A natural born huckster. The other great thing was he could take offerings by mail, through his website or by telephone. No more relying on just passing the basket amongst the pews.

Mary was one of his flock early on. She was sixteen, the daughter of a horse breeder who insisted that his children attend Sunday school, the regular church service, and Wednesday evening prayer meetings, though he never stepped into the church himself. Luke thought her father saw the church as a handy way of watching over his kids while he took time for fishing and playing with his third wife.

Mary was anxious to learn, ready to get away from her father, and soon working to please Luke in any way he might suggest or that she could think of on her own. They married when she was seventeen and had their first child—a miracle baby—Luke proclaimed, six months later. The miracle baby died of the mysterious "crib death" at eight months. He hadn't planned on having children anyway so they had no more.

Mary took to the church as fervently as had Luke. She organized fund raising drives, counseled some of the women in the congregation, and set up a missionary program that she participated in herself. Luke sometimes thought she would like to try and take over the operation of the church and step into his spot if anything happened to him or he decided to retire.

She wanted to be him and had even written her own sermons, hoping he would let her take over one day a week. It never happened. She didn't have the gift and the feedback was that she was boring. He briefly considered making her an assistant pastor, but that was a political decision as in any organization that brought in volumes of money. Lots of people wanted to fill those slots and they were used as rewards for those who could help the cause.

The case of the serial killer had stalled as far as Luke's contacts knew. There were no leads and the detectives on the joint task force were now tracking down all the background they could find on all the victims and their families. Luke hadn't thought through what would happen when they didn't solve the case right away. He had been anxious to get back to his ministry while the police looked elsewhere. Could the investigation reach out to him?

What else could he do? If he knew the identity of the killer from the HumanPestControl website he could make an anonymous call turning him in; but then what if the guy implicated him? People cut deals all the time to get their own sentence reduced. He still thought it might have been someone at the fundraiser. He could get the guest list but didn't want to raise suspicions. But a hired killer wasn't the type to run in those circles and would never have been invited. It wasn't a ball-game where you could buy a ticket from a scalper.

It was unlikely he could suggest anything that the investigators hadn't already done. But why stir up the mud when they weren't on to him? No, the best case scenario would be finding out who the contract killer was and have him killed on the spot, not arrested. Maybe catch him in the act doing a new killing. Could he set the guy up? Pay him for a new hit and have the police waiting? Or was it possible to hire another killer to take out the first one? But then he'd have the same problem with the new guy.

He wondered if he would be able to contact the killer again. Maybe the guy was scared off what with the serial killer deal going on that he knew wasn't him. Maybe the guy was even thinking the same thing and was coming after him. Luke was a public figure, so not hard to find. He made a point of portraying the church as open and available to all. A sanctuary. So he was vulnerable.

At this point the best bet would be setting the killer up. If he could find him again. The website had been closed down, but maybe if he found a way to send money that his people could trace to its ultimate destination then he could locate the guy. He had his own offshore accounts so he knew how it worked. His bank contacts in Venezuela, where the killer's money had been sent, he found out, might be able to help. For a fee of course. Everything was about money.

There were investigators he could hire but there could be unanswerable questions. Luke knew about attorney-client privilege but wasn't sure he could confide in his high-priced law firm and didn't dare use his staff lawyers. No one wants to protect murderers and that was what Luke knew they would think he was. Even though he had done a good thing in getting rid of evil scum like Earl and Mo, and even though he was sure he had been forgiven for Jerry, it was unlikely anyone would be sympathetic. There was nothing more popular that seeing the mighty fall. America's favorite entertainment. So he would contact his bankers. They seemed to have no scruples. Money talks.

9

Most people would be glad to receive an unexpected fifty thousand dollar deposit in their bank account. Not Sydney. It was a new account and she had not given out the account numbers to anyone. When she accepted a contract the client had to send the money via a wire transfer. But she hadn't taken on any new clients lately. So what was the money for and who had sent it? And it wasn't fifty thousand. It was fifty thousand minus the normal bank commission.

The bank must know what was going on and had some explaining to do. It was not a bank error in her favor, they had breached her security. She would find out from where the money originated and settle this. It was not free money. It was a message. A possibly dangerous message.

Sydney made the call to the foreign bank mid-day since she wasn't sure what time it was in Caracas. The late President Hugo Chavez had made the odd decision to change Venezuela's time zone by setting all clocks back a half-hour. This was confusing to those who dealt with the country, but not many in the US did, so it wasn't a major issue. Except to someone like Sydney and Luke, who used the country's poor relations with the US to exploit its bank's secrecy laws for funds-transfer purposes.

Her bank contact called her back, presumably on their secure line. Sydney knew her line was secure, and after much apology, and an offer to refund the commission, the banker gave up Luke's information. He knew Sydney by reputation and thought her the least desirable of the two to have as an enemy. She knew the protocol and offered the additional five percent for his help. In the Middle East it would be called baksheesh. She wasn't sure if there was a Spanish word for a polite, not quite legal, but expected bribe. There should be.

She could send the money back to Luke now. But big decisions should not be quick decisions. So she conferred with Oscar.

He was polishing his Mustang out back under the new carport. He had torn down the old rotting one, along with an old shed and a dead tangerine tree and put up a four-car covered parking space. This after she bought both of them classic '65 Mustangs as a celebration for the successful outcome of a big case a while back. He still drove his ten-year-old Buick most of the time, and she her Harley, but they both liked their Mustangs and drove them on special occasions.

Hers was souped-up, customized, and supercharged. Both were convertibles. His was a carefully restored original, with what he called, "matching numbers", a phrase Sydney didn't correct, since she knew that there was no such thing for his car but didn't want to seem like a know-it-all.

Oscar's father had originally been the one to instill the love of the classic car in him and he talked sometimes of riding in dad's old convertible as a child. Having an original was, she thought, a way of bringing his father back to Oscar a bit. She was more partial to late model BMW's but she had caught the bug and loved her version of the car for itself.

"When you get done with yours, mine could use a good rub-down too."

"Ha. Wax your own car. The only thing I'll rub down is you." He kept working, applying the soft yellow wax in a circular swirl, one section at a time, then buffing out the sections that had dried. "So what's up? Anyone minding the store?"

"I closed the gallery for the day. That's why we have

the sign: *Closed For The Day*. I need your take on something. What do I do when somebody sends me fifty thousand dollars that I don't want?"

He stopped polishing. "Now that is a problem that I have never had. What's the story?"

"This guy, Pastor Luke. He's trying to fuck with me."

"That can be very dangerous, as he should know by now."

"He sent me this money that I shouldn't have gotten. Somehow he bribed the bank officer to get it to me. It pisses me off. I'm not sure what to do about Luke. Ignoring him and keeping the money is one way. But he clearly meant this as a message. He wants me to contact him, but doesn't know who I am or have any other way to get to me. I closed down my website. But this is a security breach and the guy is pushing me further than I like to be pushed."

"Why not contact him and find out what he wants? Information is better than guessing. If he's a genuine threat then you will know better what to do."

"I can do that. But I'm afraid of a set-up. Maybe he's working with the police. Or maybe it's the police doing it. Anyway, I closed down all my Venezuela accounts and I'm transferring everything two more steps down the banking line to be safe. But you're right. I'll check him out. I'm thinking it's getting too scary around here. We may have to move on."

"He can't know much. You're totally anonymous."

"It's not just him. That judge recognized me right through the disguise. Maybe it means nothing. She isn't a cop and isn't investigating anything. But I don't like loose ends."

"I don't think of Sylvia as a loose end," Oscar said. "Maybe a corroborating witness if everything else falls apart, but not a danger in and of herself."

"She seems loose enough to me."

To make the call to Luke, Sydney had to get another burn phone. The tenth this year. That meant getting into another disguise and driving at least fifty miles to make the purchase. Nowadays if she used any cell phone and the person she called had it monitored, the police could find out when and where it was purchased, access the store security cameras, and have a picture of the buyer.

Security was getting more and more complicated. And she had to make the call from somewhere else too, using the electronic voice app on her IPad and running it through the burn phone.

She borrowed Oscar's Buick to make the run. It was ubiquitous enough to blend in, unlike her Harley Sportster that some might remember. Plus it was difficult to wear a disguise and still use the bike. This time she chose something simple. A short blond wig, flip-flops, loose white shorts, a Florida Gators T-shirt, sunglasses, and ball cap. Even Oscar wouldn't recognize her in that getup. She got off the main road and stopped at a party store named "Cold Beer", the windows of which were so covered with Florida Lottery signs and beer ads that it was difficult to see inside.

It was a poor neighborhood where many could not pass the credit check and credit card requirements to qualify for a regular cell, so there were lots of options for a burn phone. She paid cash and bought two, got cards for the minimum minutes allowed, then went outside to program one of them. It had just enough charge on the battery to complete the job. She wrote down its number and shut it down. The other she saved for next time, since there was likely to be a next time.

She had to assume Luke was a danger to her. His tactics were a clear message that he wanted to talk. But about what? Could he imagine she would take another contract from him?

10

Sydney made the call. He was playing her, she knew, but she had her own plan to deal with him. He probably felt in the comfortable position of calling the shots now. She had come to him as she knew he had hoped. She could have just kept the money and Luke wouldn't have known what to do, but she had to know what he was thinking and how far he would push her involvement in the killings.

He was the ultimate wild card and she had no information on who else he might have involved. The call was brief and scrambled as before. The caller ID would say "unknown caller", but she knew he would pick up. The ethereal voice she used this time was neither male nor female, of no particular culture or nationality, with no distinguishing accents.

"Luke, Luke, Luke," the voice said. "What are you up to now? You seem to have made us into serial killers. I don't like that much."

"What are you talking about? We have to work together..."

"Listen carefully to me since I will say this only once," Sydney interrupted. Maintaining control of the conversation was important. "I want you to take a little trip. It won't take long. You remember where you were raised don't you? Sebastian? Go there to Pearl's Fish Market, right near where your daddy and uncle docked their boat. There's a pay phone out by the road. It will ring at noon tomorrow. I would very much appreciate your being there to answer it. I need to see you in person. And I can't stress enough how important it would be for you to be alone, without any bugs or transmitters, or even a cell phone."

"Why did you choose that place? I haven't been there in

years," Luke said. "For all I know there's a condo complex there now. I'm not going anywhere. We need to put this whole thing to rest. Don't poke the hornet's nest. The police are investigating the wrong track and I want it to stay that way. They aren't going to find you and don't suspect me. The money is just to assure you that I am on your side and to make a down payment on your next job."

"I like to think of the cash as a bonus thank you for a job well done. So it hasn't bought you anything. Be there or you won't be getting a call next time. It will be a personal visit from someone you don't know and won't suspect at a time that will surprise you. And only I decide what jobs I take."

Sydney had done her homework and knew as much as anyone about Luke's history. It wasn't hard to find out his background since on his website he trumpeted his rise from a poor fisherman's son to head of the soon-to-be mega-church.

"You think I'm stupid? This is so clearly a set-up. I go to the phone and get shot. Or the telephone explodes. Or a truck runs me down. No. I won't do it. Explain yourself. What is it you want? And why should I drive all the way over there? What's the point?" He talked fast and Sydney wondered if he was sitting down or pacing. Pacing, she decided.

Sydney hesitated. What did she want? She wanted closure. She wanted to play with Oscar and her bonsai. Take Jesse for a walk. The police off her track. She wanted to know that Luke was the one that put them there. Then what? Killing him may not make the police go away. But it might eliminate leads. Or not. Who knew what he had done or whom he had told? She needed to keep him under control and sending the money to her was an act of desperation.

Desperate people made bad decisions. She couldn't have even one percent of her fate in the hands of an irrational man. She needed to make him follow her directions. Do what she said to do. It was a way of establishing dominance as well as intimidating him. And it really was a test to see if he would try to take her out. How desperate was he?

"I could kill you at any time. Even while you sit in your cozy office. But I need to see you face-to-face. Just to assure myself that I am actually talking to you and not someone pretending to be you. It's a matter of confirmation. Then I'll know neither you nor I are being set up and that we both can rely on the other to keep our secret for our own self-protection. Be there. It's your only alternative. You don't want me to jump to the wrong conclusions. You have to realize that in the end it is not in my best interest to do you any harm. I just need some reassurance."

11

The caller hung up and Luke threw the phone down. He didn't like being trumped and wasn't used to being told what to do. But what was the choice? He had trained himself to look at all alternatives, weigh pros and cons and choose the best option. He was left with only one and it was filled with uncertainty and possibly danger.

He was not to be bested. The appointment would be kept. But he would take a gun and a cell phone that he would keep turned off so it wouldn't be detected. And arrange for backup. Luke began making preparations. He wrote down everything he knew about the killer including the old website address and the information on the wire transfers. These he placed in an envelope in his personal safe that even Mary did not know how to open.

If anything happened to him his attorney had the combination and could turn over everything to the police. They might be able to kill him, but he would get his revenge. The possible embarrassment to his wife and congregation would be of no consequence to him if he died. Revenge that he knew would be carried out in the event of his death, however, would be some consolation while he lived.

The drive to Sebastian took Luke an hour and a half all during which he gripped the steering wheel with white knuckled anger. The traffic on I-95 was fast and careless. He read in the papers of someone being killed on the freeway every week. Even the construction zones had a speed limit of seventy so rush hour was not for the faint of heart. To be safe he kept pace with whatever speed the right hand lane was going, only passing if the vehicle in front was going five miles or more under the speed limit. Still, this wasn't fast enough for most of his fellow travelers as they honked, gestured, and cut him off.

Sebastian exit one-fifty-six seemed like it would never arrive. But finally he was off the fast road and he relaxed a bit heading east toward the ocean and his date with the telephone. What the killer didn't know was that he still had friends in Sebastian. Good friends. Dangerous friends. They had helped him out in the past and he had helped them even more. He had called in all his debts to be sure he held control of the table. The killer had made a mistake picking Sebastian as the meeting place.

12

Sebastian is still home to a handful of commercial fishermen, though they were outnumbered now by the charter captains who took tourists out to the reefs to catch memories to take home. There was a sort of hierarchy to the fishermen. Those in the lowest rung were the part-time inshore cast-netters who plied the Intracoastal shallows throwing their nets for mullet they sold for a dollar or so a pound.

Some would ignore the law and set out illegal gill nets at night for the high-priced and high-demand pompano and snapper, then hide the nets and claim the catch was cast-netted. Everyone knew the pompano were too fast to be caught with a cast-net, but the fish wholesalers and restaurateurs didn't ask pointed questions. The fisherman's word was good enough for them when the catch-of-the-day was involved. And the fishermen needed the money so conservation came second.

Most of the commercial fishing was done offshore, a few using hook and line, and the rest nets. There weren't any shrimpers left in Sebastian, and the oyster beds were gone, but there was a comeback in commercial clam farming. So it was a mixed bag and iffy way to make a living. Still, there were fewer fish and fewer fishermen each year.

Pearl's had been around since before Luke was born. The original Pearl was long dead, but his fish shack on the edge of the river (which is what the locals called the Intracoastal, though technically it was a saltwater lagoon) had not changed. When a board rotted it was replaced. When the roof blew off during a hurricane a new one in the same style and material was hammered in place. Crates of fish were brought to the dock by boat or to the ramp at the front of the building by pickup. Pearl's had a large walk-in cooler and made its own ice. The fish were stored until they could be shipped out in plastic tubs or sold retail to the locals.

Most of the population of the town lived west of US-1 in large subdivisions of two and three bedroom concrete-block ranch homes. The downtown, which was just a few short blocks of shops and restaurants, was at the intersection of US-1 and County Road 512, which was four lanes running due west to I-95, subdivisions flanking it north and south. It was not an affluent area. Luke's old family home near the river had been torn down several years ago to make room for a K-mart that was now vacant.

Luke arrived early and walked around the grounds near Pearl's. He hadn't been there in fifteen years but it was the same. The hard-packed shell and sand lot, tin-sided fish shack, boats on blocks in the yard that looked like they would never again feel the water, and a few sorry looking cabbage palms skirting the edges. The telephone booth was still there, by the street at the corner of the property in the bright sun next to the sidewalk.

It wasn't really a booth any longer; just a telephone box mounted inside clear plastic shielding on a steel pole. The parking area was open to the two-lane road following the edge of the river. There was an empty lot across the street and something he hadn't seen before, a new fancy restaurant and condo complex next door, right on the water. The parking lot across from it was nearly filled with cars, and people walked in groups across the street to the restaurant and gift shop.

A sign out front advertised the name of a band, *Free Beer Tonight*, which Luke thought was a creative idea for drawing a crowd to the patio bar.

The owner of Pearl's recognized him not just from his television show but from the old days. He was the age Luke's father would have been had he lived. His red hair was long and stringy, he was unshaven, and had a huge beer gut covered by a large yellow rubber apron. They talked while Red filleted and skinned a stack of mullet on the galvanized table. He sliced the fish, pushed the entrails into a bucket, sharpened his knife, filleted it, skinned the fillets, stacked them, washed everything down with a hose, and repeated, all automatically as he talked. When he finished with a fish carcass he threw it out the window into the water where a dozen white pelicans, diving seagulls, and swarms of hard-headed-catfish fought for the prize.

"Haven't seen anybody unusual hanging around," Red answered. "Just the usual bunch of fucking tourists. That place next door is a pain in the ass. They think I'm some kind of attraction, like Disney. Come in here with their kids, asking questions, getting into things. Course they ain't buying any fish. Just wasting my time and getting in the way. I ignore them and they give up. Sometimes they tell me I'm rude when they leave."

"Well, you are rude," Luke said.

"Rude is telling them to get the hell off my property. I'm polite until I find out they ain't customers. Anyway, you still need some backup?"

"I would appreciate it. Probably nothing's going to happen, but it'd be good if you covered me. I am in no way going to agree to get in a car so watch for that. If I point right at someone, shoot the bastard."

Red took his bloody apron off, rinsed his hands then flipped the Open sign on the screen door to Closed. He lifted an old bolt-action military rifle with a scarred wooden stock from behind the counter.

"I can still shoot the ass off a gnat with this. Don't

worry." He racked the bolt to chamber a round.

It was nearly noon. Luke went outside. He stayed close to his car, then walked over to the side of the property near a worn and broken wooden fence and made his way to the telephone. There was no way to get to the phone and still stay under cover. No doubt the killer planned it that way. He waited for it to ring, standing close by but behind a palm trunk in the shade. He also waited and watched for anything else that might happen.

A couple came out of the restaurant, obvious tourists in their gaudy Hawaiian shirts, athletic shoes, shorts, and straw hats. The top of her head only came up to the man's shoulder and of course everybody, even Luke, wore sunglasses under the glaring sun. It looked like they were going to visit Red. More unwanted company. He wouldn't like that. Luke considered telling them the place was closed, but the sign was there. He watched and they went inside anyway.

Ten more minutes. No call and it was overdue. The couple had come and gone, slamming the fish house door when they left. Red no doubt having told them to get the hell out of his place.

Finally the phone rang. It wasn't the same garbled voice. It was a woman with a British accent.

"Luke. I am so glad that you could make it. Sorry about the late call."

"Where are you? You said we were going to meet."

"No, I said I was going to see you and I did." The voice then changed to Darth Vader. "I was disappointed though that you didn't seem to trust me. So I had to take some action to protect myself." The voice changed again to that of a male with a mid-eastern accent. "So I found out what I need to know. And before you leave you'll find out what you need to know: that I am very serious and you should forget you ever contacted me."

The phone went dead. Luke looked around. The only people he had seen other than Red were the two tourists. Was the big guy the killer? He went back to the fish house, kicking up dust thinking how he had wasted half a day for nothing.

Red wasn't there. Maybe in the toilet. He called out. No answer. Then he stepped around the counter. Red was on his back on the wet concrete floor in a pool of blood, the rifle next to him. His mouth was open. The fillet knife was shoved into his left eye up to the hilt.

PART THREE

1

If you know someone is prepared to kill you, a wise course of action is to eliminate that possibility. That was the simple part of Sydney's complex thought process that guided her in dangerous times. Oscar and she hadn't intended to kill Red when they walked into Pearl's Fish House, they were just checking for possible witnesses and surveillance cameras before approaching Luke.

The sign said closed, but it was just an unlocked screen door and they saw movement inside so they walked right in playing pushy tourists. But Red reacted in the wrong way. Perhaps they startled him, but he pulled the old Enfield up, aimed it toward them and asked what the fuck they thought they were doing.

Oscar beat her to the punch this time. He knocked the gun out of his hands. But Red, like a lot of fat men, was very strong and got Oscar in a bear hug from behind, lifted him off his feet, and squeezed until Oscar couldn't breathe. That was when Sydney quickly grabbed the fillet knife and ended the confrontation.

Red hit the floor heavily, blood spurting from around the blade of the imbedded knife painting Oscar's head and back with warm spurting redness. Sydney washed him down quickly with the hose from the fish cleaning table, trying to keep him as dry as possible, then they walked quickly out the door and away, keeping Oscar's wet shirt out of Luke's sight. He wouldn't talk about what happened on the drive home, and that told her he was upset. Debriefing even a night on the town was his custom. They would talk about it eventually, but it would be when he had worked it all out in his mind.

"Well, now we know Luke is dangerous," Oscar finally said.

"And so far he doesn't know who either of us are. He will likely conclude that the two tourists killed the fish guy. Who else could it have been? But I doubt he could pick either of us out of a lineup."

"Have you ever been in a lineup?" Oscar said. "I've seen a few when I was doing criminal defense work and the police can set it up so the witness will pick out whoever they want picked out. But there's no way we could be identified to even be questioned, much less be suspects."

"I want it to stay that way. We need to find out more about Pastor Luke. The first murder was of Jerry, one of Luke's parishioners. That couldn't be a coincidence. We need to find out who did it. Luke might be the murderer or he might be covering for someone. While I wouldn't mind doing it, I can't just take Luke out without knowing what other people might be involved and what they might know."

"Solving a murder isn't something you're used to, is it?" Oscar said.

"No. I'm usually the problem to be solved, not the solver. But the skills transfer, so let's see what we can do."

Back in West Palm Oscar made arrangements to have the gallery staffed by Rosa, a local artist who had gotten one of her paintings into the show. He insisted on paying her for the time, but she volunteered to do it for free if she could paint while on duty. Sydney began gathering the supplies needed to go on the investigative mission. She loaded three boxes into the trunk of the Buick, changed its license plate with one from her room, and picked the type of clothing to pack for what she thought would be no more than a week-long trip.

The boxes contained: one remote control drone mini-helicopter with built-in video camera, night vision goggles (2 pair), laptop computer (new), twenty-five thousand dollars in cash, two hundred feet of mooring rope, four rolls of duct tape, four balanced and weighted throwing knives, one .223 Bushmaster assault rifle with night vision scope and ammunition, one break-down crossbow with six hunting tipped bolts, two nine-millimeter semi-automatic pistols with ammunition, one 4-ounce bottle of pentobarbital with two syringes, one cigarette-pack-size GPS transmitter with magnetic attachment, a vial of ten two-milligram tablets of Xanax crushed to powder along with several dissolvable clear envelopes, two tiny video cameras, six button sized transmitters, one remote parabolic laser microphone, one electric lock pick, and one twelve-pack of bottled water. Everything she would or might need. Oscar surveyed the contents.

"You could take over a small Central American country with this stuff."

"Not quite, but we would sure get someone's attention."

She went to see Gloria, her hair-dresser, later that day. Having her long hair cut short was not as traumatic as Sydney expected. It was a business decision. Disguises would be easier if she didn't have to worry about covering her hair and the shorter hair couldn't get grabbed, snagged, or obscure her vision in a confrontation. Gloria was horrified and tried to talk her out of it. Sydney couldn't tell her the real reason.

She just said she wanted a change, so Gloria reluctantly gave her a slick boyish cut. Wigs came in all colors and styles giving her more options at disguise. She could even dress as an effeminate male. She wasn't sure how Oscar was going to take it—he often complemented her hair and she knew men liked the look, so she decided to go with tough love. Put it in his face and see what happens.

He arrived home from another meeting with Roy and Sydney waited until he was settled in to confront him. She had ended up with a short stylish cut, not shaved to the skin but only about two inches long. With her makeup and a nice combing she thought it looked okay. Oscar was on the upstairs balcony and she said nothing, just sat in the adjoining chair overlooking the street.

"Are we ready to go?" he asked, not looking her way.

"All packed. You?" Sydney said.

"Ready to go. Just have to get a haircut so mine looks as good as yours."

She punched him in the shoulder and smiled. "How did you see me?"

"I looked down the stairwell when you came in." He turned to her and looked closely, moving his head side to side. "Sexy as hell. You busy for the next twenty minutes?"

"More like five if I know you."

They left for Orlando early the following morning. It was a three hour drive and rush hour was three hours long.

The first stop was to secure lodging. Not knowing what their schedule might be, they didn't want to end the day searching for a hotel room. Oscar booked a Hilton for five days and got upgraded to a two-room suite. Sydney wasn't impressed. She walked through the rooms. Two big-screen televisions, high-speed internet, a bathroom as big as her former New York apartment, couch, living room.

"Okay. This is terrific, but we're not going to move in here. A hotel is for sleeping and… well you know what I mean. It seems like a waste of resources."

"You mean cash? The upgrade was free, something

about Hilton points. Anyway it's nice. If you aren't comfortable here I can get you a place at the Hideaway Inn we passed. Only twenty-nine dollars a night, but I think you have to bring your own sheets and insecticide."

"Hah. Okay, but I'm ordering room service tonight, so warm up your credit card."

They left no luggage at the hotel and proceeded to Roy's Orlando office. Their luggage was not the sort to be seen by maids.

"When was the last time you went to Disneyland?" Oscar asked as they passed yet another billboard.

"Let's see, that would be never."

"Not even as a kid?"

"Oscar, I told you about my childhood. Disneyland was not in the cards. I spent my time trying to feed myself after my parents died." She stopped talking, not wanting to continue the story that Oscar had heard.

"I've never been there either. I grew up near Detroit and the closest we got was Cedar Point, an amusement park on Lake Erie. Nothing at all like what I understand Disney is about. I would go but I don't like standing in lines and being jammed together with thousands of tourists and their children, which I understand is half the experience. So what do you say, want to try it?"

"I think when I go it will be in the winter."

"Why winter?"

"Because it will be a cold day in hell when that happens."

They worked their way downtown through heavy traffic and found street parking. Roy's Orlando office took up an entire floor in a downtown office building overlooking the cityscape and the infamous sculpture "Tower of Light" in front of city hall. Its four hundred sixty-three thousand dollar cost and sixty-three foot height put a lot of people off.

Some of the critics were especially annoyed when a reviewer compared it to the Eiffel Tower. It wasn't that great. Plus it took a while to get the lights on the glass structure to work properly, but Oscar liked it. It was a bit gaudy, but given the Disney domination of the area the sculpture was certainly not out of place.

They were expected. Oscar introduced Sydney as his legal assistant. She wore a business suit and dark framed glasses with clear lenses. Rather than a note pad she carried a small notebook computer. They were taken to the local partner's corner office, all glass on the outer walls.

Juanita Ortega said she had been with the firm for four years, and had been inherited by Roy when he took over the firm. Her staff was four attorneys, four paralegals, and six office clerks. Orlando was in the center of the state and a major population center but this branch office was not as big as the one in West Palm. Oscar and Roy had discussed whether this high volume personal injury firm was the type of operation he should involve himself in, but Roy was ambitious and treated the firm as a business rather than a profession.

He was not popular with most of the ninety thousand plus attorneys in the state because of his business model. He advertised heavily on billboards, television, radio, direct mail, even the paper placemats in diners. Call an 800 number and anywhere in the state one of his attorneys was ready to help. They even did home and hospital visits. No recovery, no fee. No upfront costs. If you've been injured in any way, call Roy first.

He had been initiated into the practice by Big Jack

Burdine, who was even more outrageous and went too far, eventually dying in an explosion while on the run from the law after involving himself in an insurance fraud scheme. So Roy took over and was running it ethically and profitably. His partners and associates shared the wealth so had nothing bad to say about him. Oscar turned down the chance to be a part of it, preferring to practice law on the fringe areas and enjoy his gallery.

They sat on facing couches around a small coffee table.

"So tell me what we can do for you," said Juanita. "Frankly, we don't need any help and I suspect you aren't here to work on the bus accident case. So what is it you want and how soon will you be going home?" She had her arms folded across her chest, and leaned back in her seat.

"You cut right to the quick don't you?" Oscar said. He leaned forward and smiled and she smiled back, not too warmly, but unfolded her arms. Progress. Sydney studied her computer screen.

"We are working on a case that involves your defendant, the Gracious Lord Temple. The case isn't ready to file yet. We're in the investigative stage, but thought it helpful if we could get inside the church and perhaps talk to some of their people, maybe even the head pastor, Luke Anger. I've been contacted by the mother of one of the murder victims, the boy Jerry Prado. His mother Nancy isn't blaming Pastor Luke for the death—yet. She's a devout follower of the Pastor, snakes and all. She just wants to see if any of the other church employees might be involved since Jerry's whole school and social structure involved the church and their personnel."

"The operation is practically a cult." Juanita said. "I would hardly even call the place a church. They play with snakes and drink weak poisons to prove that God loves them. Crazy."

"I haven't taken the case yet, but agreed to investigate to see whether there is any cause of action against any other parties that might have been involved. So far it just looks like a horrible murder. But sometimes things turn up. Maybe it was an employee or one of the lay pastors. We know Jerry and his mother were deeply involved in their activities."

"The pastor is protected by levels of gatekeepers," Juanita said. "We had to depose him to get him to talk to us, but he had clearly been coached. Just gave us short answers and volunteered nothing. He has lawyers on staff so they don't care how much time they put into this and neither does he. Plus he has mucho insurance and those lawyers are also tough to deal with. So getting him to see you personally is not going to be easy. You're going to have to come up with some kind of ruse."

"And another sad thing you may have heard about," Juanita said. "Jerry's father, Clint. He was an Iraq war vet. Disabled. Lost both legs to a roadside bomb. Clint apparently couldn't deal with Jerry's death. He committed suicide."

"Suicide? When did this happen?" Oscar said.

"Just the day before yesterday. It was on the local news, him being a veteran and all."

"How do they know it was suicide?" Sydney said. She had extensive experience in making homicide look like suicide so was suspicious.

"Self-inflicted gunshot to the head while lying in bed. Between us, I think the police were happy with that conclusion. Grief is a good motive for doing yourself in, case closed. The medical examiner said it was suicide and so there was only cursory investigation. An easy explanation for an overworked department and a victim who was not going to be missed. The detective in charge said Lance Corporal Clint Prado was a gangster even if he was a war veteran. He had come back to the states, couldn't get work of course and even in his condition got involved in drug sales with some iffy people. He was awaiting trial on one charge and the only reason he made bail was they didn't think he could run far. I think the police were happy to close the case and weren't troubled if it turned out one of his business associates killed him."

"I'm going to go see the pastor. We have a lot to talk about," Oscar said.

"Let us know what we can do on this end. I don't know exactly what you'll find. Keep us in the loop and do your damndest. Here are your cards." She handed over two short stacks of business cards. "We will confirm you are of counsel to the firm if anyone calls to check on you."

"Have you learned anything about Luke Anger himself that might help us?"

"We have one case that settled and it was pretty clear he should have had criminal charges filed. But that wasn't our call. Other than that and the public information, the only stuff we have is rumor and innuendo." She leaned forward. "We have heard about his taste for the boys and girls in the congregation. We know there were allegations of inappropriate sexual situations and payoffs to shut people up. But we can't release anything because of non-disclosure agreements that came along with the settlements.

"The fact is, and we know it's true even if it's not public record, the pastor has trouble keeping it in his pants and isn't particular as to the sex or age of his victims. The other thing is that his wife seems to be the controlling force. She's always there at official functions or press conferences. Right at his elbow and they whisper back and forth if a tricky question comes up. She must know what's going on. That's about it. The rest you can find on the internet as to his history and such.

The guy has such an ego I'm surprised he hasn't written an autobiography, 'My Incredible Life So Far'. He thinks he's untouchable but we have the courts to call him to account."

They thanked her and left to confer over lunch. A game plan had to be devised before they approached the pastor.

"It seems to me that we have to explore and exploit his weaknesses." Sydney peeked inside the bag of potato chips that came with her sandwich at Bronigan's Café, then set it aside.

"The weaknesses I see, in addition to the fact that he is the likely murderer of Jerry, are two," Oscar said. "Not wanting his sex crimes to come out in the open, if Juanita is right about that, and protecting his empire."

"Both of those amount to the same thing. But we don't know much about the wife, Mary."

Sydney picked the chips back up and tasted one, then put the bag back down. "I think you can eat just one, regardless of what the advertising tells you."

"Let's step back a minute. I think the trees are obscuring our view of the forest. What exactly is our goal here? We already know that the pastor is guilty of something or he wouldn't have had that guy with the rifle ready to shoot us. And we know he paid to have the other two guys eliminated."

"And," Sydney said, putting the bag of chips on Oscar's tray, out of temptation's reach, "we think he did it to cover up killing number one. What we don't know for sure is whether he was killer number one, even though he probably is, or maybe it's the wife, and we don't know how to get the police to look at him without digging into our involvement. Maybe he's trying to cover for someone else. If he confessed he would implicate us for sure.

"If we killed him the police would likely still be looking for us. Other people, Mary for instance, may know about him hiring Human Pest Control. I think the website is opaque, but who knows when you're safe if you're potentially dealing with the FBI?"

"It looks like I need to go on this fishing expedition to the church and see what's biting," Oscar said. Then he finished the bag of chips.

"I've already laid groundwork for becoming a member. I could visit again if it would help in any way. If we can get enough evidence to convince the police to pin all the murders on Luke or whoever's working with him it would take the heat off us."

2

Sydney called the church office to make an appointment with the pastor. Initially the request was refused. She had to use their cover story: that Oscar was part of Roy's legal team which supposedly represented an unnamed minor who parents had approached them about allegations of sexual misconduct by a church official. Oscar wanted to see if the story was legitimate or if the child had even been a member of the church before agreeing to take the case. The secretary called back and gave him fifteen minutes at three that afternoon. If what Juanita said was true, the pastor would be accustomed to settling cases of this kind.

"Maybe you should wait in the car. You don't want to be recognized." Oscar drove down the two lane crumbling asphalt bordered by low palmettos and cattle fields.

"Look at me. Do you think I'd be recognized?" She had slicked back her newly short hair, parted it on the side, and wore a white blouse with a dark blue jacket that flattened her unbra'd breasts, matching blue pants, and open-toed leather sandals.

"I guess not. You have that cute androgynous look."

Getting onto the church grounds required going past a security checkpoint on the way in. A post with a key pad was on the driver's side of the entrance gate, but the gate was already open since a white-shirted guard stood inside a guard house checking the incoming visitors. Oscar whistled at the size of the gates, which slid sideways on a track to open.

"I don't think I've ever seen steel gates that massive. They must be fifteen-feet high. And spiked at the top. What is this guy protecting anyway?"

"Probably nothing," Sydney said as they drove through. "Did you notice the fencing around the property? Nothing like the gates. The concrete wall only extends a hundred feet on either side, then it's chain link. Not even barbed wire on top. I think it's all for effect. Like in the old days when banks built huge stone buildings with columns to impress the public. Make them think their money's safe."

"Yeah. And cathedrals. Impress the natives with the size of God's buildings."

After winding through the expansive grounds of the church and following the signs pointing the way to the charter school, the bus lot, and a narrow gated driveway, they drove past a Walmart sized parking lot to the left of the church building itself. The building was gigantic, but with no style. It resembled a three-story pole-barn with big windows. A cross twice the height of the building towered over a reflecting pond. The cross might have been impressive except that it was under construction and so far was half covered with what looked like white aluminum clapboard siding.

"Cheesy," said Sydney. "You'd think the pastor would spring for limestone or bronze."

They pulled into the circular driveway at the entrance and parked under the awning.

"I don't think this is a parking place," Sydney said. "It looks like they park off to the side."

"This is closest to the door, in the shade, and it's hot out there in the parking lot."

The entrance to the tabernacle was through two sets of double doors. Straight ahead was the auditorium-like worship area with rows of pews, the open gathering area and a low stage at the rear backed by red velvet curtains. Above it all was a loft area, almost a sky-box with mirrored windows looking down over the worship area. A small sign inside indicated that

Administrative Offices were to the left where another set of doors led to a reception area reminiscent of a corporate headquarters. They went left to the offices.

Original artwork was on the walls, waiting areas with black leather couches were left and right, and the reception desk was directly ahead backed by a stone wall with water trickling down it. The desk was occupied by a lone twentyish woman in a long-sleeved man-style shirt in light blue with a button down collar. She was sitting behind two computer monitors reading a book. The telephone wasn't ringing and no one else was in the waiting room.

Still, they were made to wait.

"I think the fifteen minutes they allotted us are up," Oscar said, looking at his watch.

"Here comes somebody."

A youngish man with thin black tie and an identical light blue shirt led them up a flight of open stairs to the head man's office. Apparently the handicap access laws didn't apply to his private space. When they walked in Pastor Luke Anger was at a conference table to one side, flanked by a man and a woman with paperwork on the table in front of them. They all stood when Oscar and Sydney were led in. Southern manners.

They introduced themselves all around, dealt business cards, and sat. The two flankers were the in-house attorneys. Water glasses, a pitcher of ice water and pens and pads of paper were at each place. Very corporate.

Luke leaned forward, hands clasped on the table, all smiles, brushed back blond hair, and powder blue suit.

"Now what can we do for you folks?"

"We have been asked to look into allegations of sexual impropriety concerning one of the church officials," Oscar said, mirroring Luke with a smile and clasped hands.

"I am sorry to hear that. In an organization as big as this you must know we are easy targets. We have to deal with spurious and outlandish claims every so often. People looking to make a quick buck. Just who is making this accusation?"

Oscar noted that he asked for the accuser before asking the name of the accused.

"The client is a minor and a member of the church, so for the time being I would prefer to keep the name confidential."

"Then I don't see how we can help. We will need information, don't you know. Can't squash the roach if it don't come out from under the cupboard."

Real homey, Oscar thought.

"My client wouldn't like to be thought of as a roach."

"No, no. That's not what I meant. I meant solve the problem. We take these allegations seriously but need to know what to investigate. Just what is it you want to know?" Luke had leaned back in his chair, his hands clasped over his vest covered belly.

"We are interested in your mentoring program. Who is involved and the procedures you take to oversee the mentors. Is it strictly one-on-one, or a group sort of thing? In fact it would be helpful to talk to the children being mentored and the mentors themselves. Are there field trips? Are there multiple chaperones? Are the children ever invited alone to accompany a mentor on any activity. That sort of thing." Oscar had no real hope they would give him any of the information he asked for. His point was to make this trip look legitimate.

Sydney dropped her pen on the floor while Oscar was talking, said "oops" and stuck a small audio transmitter to the underside of the table as she leaned down to get it. It was voice-activated and the batteries were good for two hours of continuous transmission; which meant a lot of time if it only switched on during intermittent talking. The bug had cell phone capability, much like a non-wired burglar alarm. When activated it sent the conversation to Sydney's IPad, where it was recorded as a message on a separate channel. If found and opened up, the circuits fried so it could not be traced.

The woman flanker spoke up. "You're being overbroad in your questions as well as over-reaching. If you have a specific complaint, we would be glad to hear it. Otherwise this is a waste of time. Who, exactly is being accused of this so-called impropriety, and what's the impropriety?"

"I try to be discreet and don't want to embarrass any-one with what may turn out to have an innocent explanation," Oscar said. "But the fact is Pastor Anger is himself the one accused of having a sexual relationship with an under-aged parishioner's child." That should stir things up, he thought.

It didn't seem to faze them. The attorneys made a point of examining their paperwork, waiting for a cue from the boss. Maybe there were multiple under-aged children who would fit the bill and they were trying to decide who he was referring to.

"You have to work on your discretion," Luke said to Oscar. "I hear all sorts of accusations and this is one of the easiest to make, the most damaging, and the hardest to disprove. It becomes my word against the child's and people are quick to form a lynch mob." He stood and walked to his desk, sitting and shuffling papers as he talked.

"I have very close relationships with the children in my flock. Counseling is an important part of my mission. Many of these children have been abused by others or are suffering from emotional problems. Frankly they are sometimes talked into believing that things happened to them that never occurred. Nonetheless, we have to deal with their accusations to protect the integrity of the church. You probably know we have settled lawsuits before, the idea being that it would be better for everyone to focus on our work here than have the Temple's name dragged through the courts and tried in the press. So we settle. It doesn't mean we admit to wrongdoing. Now I am going to ask you to leave and do not come back without a subpoena or an invitation."

With that he left the room. Oscar said he would be in touch and they retreated down the stairs.

On the drive out, they took the long way, going around the back of the building, passing narrow driveways on the right that disappeared through the trees and following the road as it circled the compound around the back of the church and past the school to end back at the main gate. There were four cars parked under an overhang out of the sun at the back door of the church. One was a new Mercedes sedan. Not likely to be the help.

"Do you think that's Luke's car?" Sydney said.

"The vanity license plates read 'GodMan1' so I think that's a good guess." Oscar pulled over, the passenger side to the Mercedes, and Sydney jumped out, opened the rear door of the Buick, fumbled with her shoulder bag and the contents spilled to the ground. She bent down and scooped them up, in the process sticking a small square box on the underside of the rear bumper of the car.

"You seem to keep dropping things. Do we have what we need in place?" Oscar drove up to the gate and it automatically slid open. He stopped on the edge of the road a hundred yards outside the grounds.

"We now have a GPS on the car that will transmit its travels to my computer. And they might still be talking inside. Let's find out." Sydney opened her IPad, tapped it to get to the appropriate app and they listened to the conversation going on inside the conference room. It started in the middle of a heated conversation.

"…can't go through this again, Pastor. You know this isn't covered by insurance. The last one we barely kept out of the papers." It was the woman attorney.

"This is my congregation and my church and you work for me. Don't forget that. I don't know what they're talking about. No one that I mentor would complain about anything and I certainly am not having any inappropriate relationships. The other times were baseless. You know we paid them off to avoid scandal, not because they could prove anything."

"They had proof enough for us to recommend settling. And you agreed then to stop the individual counseling with younger people. Has that changed?" The woman again.

"I have an obligation to my flock. They look to me for guidance. How can I refuse?"

"Who are you counseling at this time? We may need to look at damage control." The male attorney.

"There's nothing there, I tell you. I've done nothing wrong. I speak to Julie Weston about the scholarship from time-to-time, but that was on Mary's advice and recommend-dation. And she's hardly a child, she's fifteen for goodness sake. Old enough to make her own decisions on relationships. I help the children with their questions of faith and do counseling to help them deal with the heathen world and its distractions. I talk to them about the value of education. I am also helping two boys who are thinking of a career in the church so I talk to them, but that's it."

Oscar and Sydney looked at each other, speechless, and imagined the two attorneys were doing the same. Fifteen was old enough for him.

They wrapped up their talk and the microphone went dead.

"Okay. We've got a name. You got the bugs planted. We can track his movements. We have seen the layout inside and out. Now it would help if we had some physical evidence and more info."

"I may have a way of getting that, too," Sydney said. They went back to the hotel to find out all they could about Julie Weston. Sydney spent the evening using the hotel's high-speed internet and room service while wrapped up in the complementary plush hotel bathrobe. She pulled up an interactive map that followed the Mercedes, but it travelled only a short way, staying on the grounds. Probably the residence.

Julie had a Facebook page, but most information was available only to friends, so Sydney set up a fake account and tried to friend her. Some people will take all the friends they can get, so it wasn't a total long-shot. She was a victim but probably didn't realize it.

3

Another bible-rose killing had been reported, this one of Red the fishmonger. It was front page, on television and on all the news feeds. No arrests had been made. There were no persons of interest. They said again it seemed these were random killings. The governor was talking about a shake-up of the special task force. The FBI was involved. The police had tried to find DNA on the roses, but had nothing yet. Nancy Grace had switched her focus to the Bible Rose serial killer.

The bibles were another link, since they were all exactly the same, but were generic, sold all over the world on the internet and in religious book stores by the tens of thousands. None had stickers, stamps, or markings to make them different from any of the others and while fingerprints were recovered, they did not match any in the FBI database. Luke still had plenty of the bibles, and of course roses were sold everywhere.

Luke had not been re-interviewed by the police. The locals were still pursuing the investigation of Jerry's death, but since it seemed Jerry was the first of many random killings, they had removed the case from the top priority list, leaving it to the task force and its unlimited resources, with only one local detective left with the file.

Mary was dropping in to Luke's office unannounced several times a day. Luke was annoyed, since it interrupted his regular work load and because he knew why she was doing it. But he had no plans to bring Julie or anyone else up the back elevator for a tryst. At least not for a while. Julie was persistent, however, and a potential danger since she could go public. What if she was the one that the lawyer Leopold was referring to? But would she risk the scholarship? He had always done whatever was needed to protect her and keep her happy but she was needy. Still, he missed their get-togethers. Maybe she thought a cash settlement would be a bigger prize than the scholarship. She was hinting at needing money and talked about the kind of car she wanted when she got her license. A Lexus. He had to see her privately, and not in the office. Promise her a little cash bonus and feel her out. Having her disappear for good would be convenient, but the office was too close to home and he made himself think of other options.

There was the condo. The church kept it for guests who might be staying long-term to teach seminars or for out of town VIP's. It was currently vacant. Luke used the choir office telephone line to call Julie on her cell. She was in the choir so a record of the call wouldn't seem out of place. It was afternoon and she would be out of school. She answered and he arranged a meeting with her at the condo after school the next day.

He would pick her up. She had been there before and promised that she had never told anyone about it. Luke said he wanted to go over everything that had happened and work out a plan that would help both of them. She said she loved him as she disconnected.

4

Luke's side of the call had been recorded by the signal sent by the bug under the conference table via a transmission to Sydney. A dedicated tone alerted her to the new message. She relayed it to Oscar.

"We need to find out where they're meeting and listen in on Luke's description of what he calls 'everything that has happened' and find out what the plan is. Maybe we'll get lucky and get some kind of confession."

"We have the GPS. We can follow. School is usually out around two-thirty." Oscar said.

"It would be infinitely better if we knew where they were going ahead of time so we could check the place out before they got there. He said condo, but where is it? We need to make preparations of our own before they arrive."

"If this is some kind of sex hook-up…"

"You can bet on that," Sydney said.

"Then video would be terrific. We can use it as leverage. If we get him on tape having sex with a minor and confront him with it he may spill other information, maybe even fess up to Jerry's death. That could be the confession we need."

"And the police would likely get the girl's cooperation too. She may know a lot about what goes on with Pastor Luke and the other kids," Sydney said.

They went through the online database for county real estate holdings. None were in the name of Luke or Mary Anger, but the church owned a half-dozen parcels. All but one was contiguous to the church property. The other was in Winter Park.

A condo.

Winter Park is not a suburb of Orlando, as one might believe driving to it, given that the Orlando sprawl has deleted any visible dividing line. It is one of the many municipalities in Orange County that make the greater Orlando area one of the largest population centers in the country, with over two-million residents. The city itself has a population of only about a quarter-million. But then there are the tourists. Because of the theme parks created by Disney, Universal Studios, and others since 1971, over fifty-million people a year visit Orlando. So the roads, restaurants, and hotels are far more numerous and crowded than should be called for by the number of permanent residents.

The Church location on the outskirts of town was perfect for the ambitions of Luke for his Gracious Lord Temple. A fast-growing population, international airport, and numerous media outlets. Winter Park was northeast of town and was a carefully crafted tourist destination with galleries, restaurants, upscale shopping, and museums. Luke's out-of-town visitors loved the ambience and Luke loved the location because it was close to home, yet had the anonymity that comes with crowds. Perfect for his illicit liaisons.

Oscar and Sydney arrived at nine in the morning, which would give them time to set up their equipment before the expected afternoon arrival of Julie and Luke.

The condo was not one of those apartment-like habitations. It was more a townhouse in a row of eight abutting units fronting the sidewalk in a European manner with under-house parking in the back. They were all three-bedroom with two-and-a-half baths, with the master bedroom on the second floor. The church's unit was in the center of the building, though Sydney would have preferred to have found it on the end for ease of surveillance. The county real estate database even had a floor-plan of the condo on record from the tax assessing department. Very helpful.

Getting in was no problem for Sydney. She showed Oscar her key. It looked a lot like a plastic toy gun, but with a movable wire sticking out the front instead of a gun barrel.

"I used to have to pick the lock with the tools like you see in the movies. You know, tiny screwdriver-like metal picks, hooks and forks, all in a convenient pocket-sized carrying case." She pulled a set out of the bag at her feet in the van to show him.

"But technology helps even the burglar. I bought this online. If you don't believe me, Google it." She pulled the trigger of the gun-like tool and the metal tongue on the end moved in and out. "The way the pick gun works is the little finger you see moves rakes the pins inside the lock when you hold the trigger in and twist the tension bar slightly. When the right combination hits, the lock slides open. Only takes a few seconds instead of minutes, so someone walking by or looking out a window isn't going to wonder what you're doing fiddling around with the door. But it takes practice. I'm pretty good at it now but had a hell of a time making it work the first time."

"This is legal?"

"It's not legal to own in most places. Possession of burglary tools is what they charge you with. A felony. But it's legal to buy. But then you can buy virtually anything online, legal or not, and I have a secure mail drop where things like this are delivered. So no tracing me. Did you know lock-picking is a legitimate hobby and there are even national competitions? Of course you can't use a pick gun like this and win a prize. Anyway, getting in is not a problem. But that's not always the end of it. Once we're in, we have to deal with the alarm, which most places have nowadays.

"There are several kinds, including motion activated ones. But I know how to deal with most of them. What's common nowadays for those who can afford it is the wireless system that sends its call to the police via cell phone. So I have a jammer that can cancel the cell signal for enough time to get done what we need to do. If it's hard-wired or not, we know there's a one to two minute delay while the disarm code is entered. I can bypass that if I have to, but my plan is to work fast, block the audible indoor signal with some spray shaving foam inside the speaker, and be out before the police can get here. I figure I have at least four minutes, but shouldn't need that much time. The shaving cream evaporates in a while so no one will see what I did. If the alarm signal went out and the police show, it will look like another false alarm. They get a lot of those."

"Four minutes doesn't seem like much."

"You should try timing yourself doing normal things around the house. Walk outside to get the mail and come back. Probably no more than a minute. Take the clothes out of the washer and put them in the dryer then pour yourself a cup of coffee. Maybe another minute and a half. People overestimate the time things take."

"What are you going to do when you get inside?"

"I'm going to leave listening devices in the kitchen, living room, and master bedroom, along with a wireless pinhole camera covering the bed and another with an over-all shot of the living room. The cameras have a pull-off adhesive strip so they can be quickly mounted under a table-top or the bottom of a shelf so as not to be seen. I estimate two to three minutes to put everything in place and be back out. You be the lookout and text me if anyone is coming in or hanging around the front door. I may have to go out through the garage."

They had rented a white panel van for the job in Winter Park that morning, then borrowed a license plate from another white van of the same make and model in a secluded parking lot on the way. The ubiquitous white van was used as a work vehicle by every manner of service industry in Florida. Plumbers, electricians, carpet cleaners, exterminators—nearly every industry used them. White to reflect the sun, they had only two bucket seats, and were otherwise filled in the back with whatever tools the owners needed for their particular business. So they were expected, ignored, and invisible.

The laptop monitored the movements of the Mercedes by tracking the GPS on the online interactive map. They knew where it was, how fast it was going, and even could display the addresses where it might stop. If they missed something the movements were all in memory for replay.

Sydney hopped out of the van, carrying a small shoulder satchel. Her red ball-cap and short jacket had the words "Factory Service" on them by way of adhesive letters they had picked up at an office supply. Good enough to look official at a distance. Oscar parked parallel on the other side of the street a half block away. He watched as Sydney opened the door lock and deadbolt as quickly as anyone could have done with a key. None of the people on the street paid any attention, and there was no audible alarm after she closed the door. Less than three minutes later, she was out and relocking the door. They moved the van away from the condo.

She threw her hat and jacket in the back. "Let's get some breakfast."

"I'm never going to feel like my house is locked up again. What do I have to do, push furniture against a door to keep you out?"

"You don't want to keep me out sweetie." She leaned over and kissed him on the cheek. "If you want security a tumbler lock is not the way to go. Why do you think hotels have gone to the magnetic strip swipe or key pads?"

They went to a local coffee shop where laptop usage was common so they could keep tabs on the Mercedes during lunch. The car had still not moved when they left. There was a convenient parking spot in the shade near the condo adjacent to City Park. They waited, watched the graphic map for movement of the Mercedes, and listened for any sound in the condo through an earpiece in case Luke might have taken a different car. The front door of the condo was a couple of blocks off and visible, but they could not see the rear entrance.

At three-fifteen the yellow dot representing the Mercedes began to move.

"Finally. I can't stand the inaction," Oscar said.

"Let me split the screen so we can watch the inside cameras at the same time." Sydney took the laptop and punched in the appropriate code.

The dot moved slowly across the screen on an interactive map. Sydney zoomed in so they could read the street names on the map. The car stopped at one location for five minutes about halfway to the condo.

"Is it still working? Do you think he found the transmitter, or did it fall off?" Oscar turned the laptop screen toward himself a bit more.

"That's too long for a red light. Maybe he stopped at a store. You know, champagne and seduction supplies." Sydney kept her eyes on the screen.

"We have a problem. It's going the wrong way." She showed the screen with the other dot travelling on the road away from the temple. It was heading northwest.

"What the hell? Where's he going?" Oscar said.

"Maybe he has another love nest we don't know about. Could be renting rather than owning so it wouldn't show up on the property records. Or maybe she wasn't on the grounds when he left and he picked her up at the last stop."

They watched as the dot moved toward the outskirts and away from downtown. The condo was now due east of the moving car and a good fifteen miles away. It kept going, making several turns until it stopped on a minor road north of Lake Apopka, northwest of Orlando in the sticks.

"I think we need to follow it," Sydney said. "We'll pick up your car at the rental place so I've got wheels, then you go back to the condo in the van and monitor the videos when and if they arrive. I'll follow the car and see who's in it and where they're going. If it's Luke I have the equipment to improvise a surveillance and get a recording. You can use the laptop to track them and I'll follow the GPS with my phone. You can call or text me if they show up here in another car."

Sydney pulled up another window on the computer and zoomed in on the area the car had stopped. She used the web application on Google Earth which gave her a satellite image of the site as well as a ground level view of the area where the car had stopped.

"Okay. We know what was there when this satellite image was taken. The site may have changed by now but it looks like it's an abandoned industrial site with structures that appear to be old Quonset huts from the fifties. Cheap way to put up a building back then. A lot of broken pavement and scrubby trees." She flipped back to the GPS map. "The car still hasn't moved. I'm going to go run over there and see what's up."

"Let's think a bit on this. Why are we concerned about where the Mercedes went?"

"Because he's got the girl, Julie, we think. What if he's trying to eliminate her?" Oscar said.

"Or, this just might be another romantic rendezvous point. He might have called her and that Google Earth shot might have been taken two years ago. New buildings go up all the time. It could be a hotel now for all we know. Our goal here is not to save lives. It's to get the goods on Pastor Luke. Something we can use. Proof of child molestation or statutory rape would be good. But proof that he's a murderer is the only thing that will help us. I say go after him."

"Suppose the girl hasn't been killed yet, if that's his plan. Aren't we going to try and stop him?"

"Of course. She's an innocent. Maybe a little too hormoned up for her own good, but still just a kid. He's the evil one."

"Then why not just call the police? They have manpower, cars with sirens, and swat teams," Oscar said.

"Because we're making assumptions. We don't know anything except that he was planning on meeting this young woman and setting out a new plan. Maybe sex, but that's just another assumption. Do we tell the cops to go to both places? They wouldn't do anything without verifiable imminent danger. And who are we? You can be sure they will ask."

Oscar pulled away from the curb and they entered the Mercedes location in the GPS direction finder in the computer. The car rental place was on the way. The computer's estimate was a half-hour to reach the Mercedes and possibly be on time to save Julie.

5

Sydney was three-quarters of the way through heavy traffic to the target when the GPS marker moved. It back-tracked, then headed southeast, presumably to home base. Sydney updated Oscar by cell phone as she travelled.

"How long did it stay at that location?"

"Eighteen minutes."

"What do you think? Follow the car or check out the spot where it stopped?" Sydney continued toward the location, but was ready to reverse course.

"I think we need to see what's there at the least. We can still come back for the car and track it while we scope out where and maybe why he stopped," She said.

"He was there long enough to do anything. Let's hope nothing bad. We don't even know if the girl was with him."

She approached the site, passing the entrances to subdivisions on the two lane road. The countryside was wide open, hot, and dry. Occasional worn out strip malls were followed by aging small cinderblock industrial buildings with a car or two parked in the sun in front of them. A lot of sand, dust, and scruffy unkempt trees. Disney hadn't made it this far north to pristinely landscape and irrigate everything. Just past a septic tank pump-out company on the left was the side road she was looking for. The first hundred yards were paved, then it turned to sand and shell. Her car shot up a rooster-tail of white dust as it shot down the road.

Just ahead on the left was a cleared lot. It appeared just as it had on the Google image. Surrounded by a broken-down chain-link fence, the weedy concrete lot fronted a large, rusted, corrugated-steel Quonset hut. There was an overhead door pulled closed and a side door with a small cracked window. No vehicles were evident as she pulled up to the structure and the pavement would not have picked up any tire tracks.

Sydney parked to the side of the building and left the van door open with the keys on the seat. She had a nine-millimeter Glock held down next to her leg as she approached the building and stood to the side of the door. She tried to see in through the window but it was pure blackness inside. She tried the door. It was unlocked. She pulled it open and stood aside, waiting, but nothing happened, just the dusty wind whipping around her and the sun eating into her dark clothes. She stepped quickly inside, crouched, and moved to the left of the door with the gun up in both hands while waiting for her eyes to adjust.

The floor was cluttered with industrial debris. Rolls of steel cable, piles of twisted metal, big drums stacked up and filled with who-knew-what. Toward the back was what had probably been the office. A small building within a building. It was just a box with a door, a flat roof and windows on all sides. Probably where the foremen stayed and kept the noise out while the long-gone workers labored at their noisy machinery. She picked her way toward the room, on alert. There was no noise and an almost familiar smell of old oil and dust.

The door to the office room was unlocked, but it was darker inside than out. Sydney looked for a light switch, thinking the chances were slim since the place looked like it had been abandoned for years.

But the six fluorescent ceiling lights flickered on when she flipped the switch on the wall near the door, providing a dim, almost blue, light to the small space. The room was about twenty-feet square with an eight-foot suspended acoustical tile ceiling. There were four battered steel desks, still with paperwork scattered, and a half-dozen chairs standing or fallen around the room. At the back corner was what she had not wanted to find. Sydney held the gun in both hands combat style and checked her perimeter. Clear.

In the corner on the floor was a teenage girl, clothed, but unconscious and handcuffed to a pipe near the wall. Sydney put the gun away and went to her. The pulse was strong. There was a one-gallon plastic bottle of water within reach, and an empty pail. Whoever had left her would be coming back but not soon. She called Oscar, explaining the situation as she looked around for something to open the cuffs.

"I think she's been drugged. There's no apparent injury. Luke must have stashed her here. For what purpose I hate to imagine," Sydney said.

"Can you get the cuffs off her?"

Sydney rolled her eyes, "Have you got a toothpick and a blindfold?" She found a short piece of wire and unlocked the cuff on the girl's wrist. She was limp and still unconscious. "I'm taking her to a hospital."

The girl was heavier than Sydney, but she managed to get her to the van using a fireman's carry over her back. With the passenger seat all the way back and reclined she was able to get the girl into the van and fairly comfortable, She strapped her in but the girl, whom she assumed was Julie, still didn't respond. There had been no purse and a quick check produced no identification. Sydney looked for directions to the nearest emergency clinic on her phone and took off.

"How are you going to explain who you are?" Oscar asked over the cell.

"I'll use the cap and jacket. I'm with factory service. I happened on her while on a call. I'll drop her at the front desk, then get out quick before too many questions are asked. Right now would be a bad time to have the police questioning me.

I'll call in a tip on the Mercedes after I leave there.

"Any time is a bad time for the police to question you." Oscar was still watching the laptop. "The Mercedes is almost back to the church grounds."

"What do you say we meet back at the hotel and regroup? I'm kind of confused about our plan right now," Sydney said as she approached the hospital area. "Unexpected things happen. You can't plan for them. I could use a session in that spa tub to think."

"You love the tub."

Okay, I admit it. I love the room. We should redecorate the loft to match it."

Oscar left for the hotel ten minutes before Luke arrived at the condo.

6

Julie never showed. He had offered her a ride but she wasn't at the meeting site as arranged. He had to assume she was somewhere else and was taking the bus. There was no choice other than go over to the condo to see if she arrived. He even stopped on the way and bought flowers for her. White roses. And he brought a bible. What had happened? She didn't answer her cell. But it wasn't turned off and she wasn't talking to anyone else since it didn't immediately go to voicemail when he rang her.

He waited in the condo for an hour, finally cracked the Champagne and drank two glasses, tossed the roses in the dumpster in the parking lot, then returned home. Maybe someone had gotten to her. Or more likely it was her womanly way of trying to punish him for not giving her the attention she wanted. They had almost been caught and he knew the panties were not an oversight as she claimed.

She wanted their affair to be public. It would somehow make her feel important to let the world know whom she was fucking. She probably had no idea that going public would ruin him—or didn't care. He couldn't let that happen and had hoped the condo meeting would have led to an understanding. Otherwise he would have found another way to silence her. He thought he had done enough for her but seemed to get no credit for what happened or what he had done for her in the past. Money usually worked, but she had this idea she was in love, so she wasn't trustworthy. Love confused rational thinking in his view.

Mary was there when he got home. The Mercedes had been gone earlier so he had had to use the church van for the trip to the condo. He parked at the rear of the building in employee parking and took the elevator to his office, not checking in with the staff downstairs. Mary would want him to go over the script for the Sunday radio and television broadcast of his sermon. The routine was to do a taped rehearsal in the on-site studio on Saturday afternoon. Even though his sermon was ad-libbed for the most part, she wanted no gaffs when he was broadcasting. In effect, she was the producer and director of his shows.

The popularity of the fire and brimstone nature of his sermons was spreading and they were entering new markets every month. New markets meant more donations. Being a church meant no taxes, including property, sales, or income tax. He had to pay tax on his salary, but that was kept low. The church provided their home, cars, a mountain retreat in the Catskills for those hot summer days or during a hurricane emergency, the offshore yacht for educational cruises, and the retreat in Costa Rica for mission work.

They had all the trappings of wealth while being able to say to his followers when pressed that he took just a small salary with nearly all the money that the congregation tithed or donated going to church causes. Good marketing for what was in fact a big business. A long way from where he and Mary had started out. Luke wanted her to have nice things and she asked for a lot of them. While he had a small salary, Mary was paid handsomely for her duties as Director of Church Activities. Another church related expense, and a big one.

He had no idea how much she had put away over the years but suspected it was nearly everything she had been paid since all her living expenses were also paid by the church. But she needed him, he knew that. She wasn't the draw. He was the star. Luke had in the back of his mind that at some point she would have enough money and would leave him. She hadn't reached forty yet, and talked of doing things that weren't allowed to a preacher's wife.

He stood at the one-way glass, looking down into the church auditorium. If this whole mess of the killings would just go away and the Julie problem was solved, things in his life would be just about right.

The next day the Apopka police put out a photo in the Orlando papers and on the internet of Julie. "Do You Know This Girl?" the caption read, along with a short description of what the police knew. It took no time at all for her to be identified and her parents contacted the church to have someone go with them to look after her. She was hospitalized but unconscious. Whatever drug had been given to her was powerful and had not worn off. Mary volunteered to go with the family to sit vigil at the hospital.

"I want you to know, Luke, that if she recovers we are going to have a problem. And I'm not going to take the fall for trying to cover up your shit."

"What are you talking about?"

"I'm the one who kidnapped Julie. She came to me claiming you had raped her in your office. She wanted cash and a guarantee that she would get the scholarship or she would go public. I panicked. She came to the house. She was going to ruin us. I never liked that girl. I could tell she was after you. Now I know why. What could I do? She waited in the living room for me while I went to get her a drink. I crushed up a handful of my valium in the coffee grinder, mixed it in some sweet tea and gave it to her. My mind was on killing her, but she just went to sleep. So I took her out to Apopka to daddy's old machine shop. I was going to kill her there but just couldn't do it. So I left her some water, handcuffed her and came home to try and decide what to do with her."

"Handcuffed her?"

"They were Daddy's and were there so I used them."

Mary started crying, alternating with screaming at Luke that it was all his fault for being such a sex pervert. Luke convinced her to take two of her valiums to calm down.

Her inept handling of Julie had created a crisis situation. Luke had no idea how he was going to handle it. Money would have solved everything if Mary had only kept out of it but now he had lost that option. Maybe if Julie didn't wake up the problem would be solved.

7

When Oscar checked his phone there was a message from Rosa who had been watching the gallery. Detective Ramirez had stopped in earlier in the day. He wanted a meeting and had left his number. He was very insistent. So Oscar called after first considering ignoring the guy. They set a time late the next day. Ramirez also wanted to know if Oscar could arrange to have Louise there since he had been unable to contact her.

"What do you think? Should Louise meet with him?" Oscar asked Sydney.

"I have to think about the potential danger there. He will want to know where I live, and I don't have a verifiable address for Louise. I used a mail drop for my residence when I got my driving license. I have I.D., and it's good, but I would have to come up with something. Some cover. We have to ask what if. What if I didn't? Would he give up? Not likely. I would be on his list of unanswered questions and it would remain that way in the case file. What if I met with him and had an answer to where I lived? The only difficulty is if he somehow noticed I was in disguise. But all he might have at this point is a physical description and possibly some group photos from the fundraiser. I tried not to be photographed but who knows? And the only sticky part of the disguise is the wig, but it's high quality and so far as I know he's never seen Sydney. And people do wear wigs, it's not illegal. It should work."

"It would get him off our backs. Odds are he's just trying to tick you off his list."

"Yes. There's that. But Sydney would have to keep a low profile for a while. We can't have him meeting both Sydney and Louise. He's a detective after all. I'd have to be

Louise for a while."

"I don't think I ever slept with a redhead. It could be pretty exciting."

"You won't see anything new, babe."

Traffic on I-95 was the usual mix of speeding SUV's driven by homicidal road-raged cell-phone talkers and retirees with nowhere to go and no hurry to get there who liked to drive five miles below the speed limit in the left lane. Oscar preferred the side roads but didn't want to add an hour to the drive from Orlando so was forced to fight both groups. It was a relief to get back.

He checked in with Rosa who was painting in front of an easel at the back of the gallery.

"No customers today," she said. "But there was a woman in yesterday who said she was coming back to buy sometime this week. A judge somebody. I didn't catch it. Other than that, it's been nice and quiet."

"Judge Pocholi?"

"That could be it."

Oscar wanted Rosa gone before Ramirez showed, so he sent her home. Sydney went into her office and did whatever she did back there, usually on the computer. They had stopped at a Publix Food Store after leaving the interstate and stocked up on fresh food and coffee, which Oscar made in the downstairs pot.

Sydney had agreed to be Louise for the interview in an effort to help the detectives close her part of the file. The story would be that she had been staying with a friend until she could get her own place and had been modeling for Oscar and picking up work where she could. She actually had a friend that agreed to cover for her.

"It's my hairdresser, Gloria." She was in the middle of the makeover to becoming Louise. No wig or contacts yet, but she had on Louise type clothes. The familiar South Florida costume: Athletic shoes, white shorts, pastel blouse, and if it was chilly, a sweater tied around either the shoulders or waist. Jewelry was required, usually at least a bracelet and necklace. Makeup too.

A total non-Sydney look. Sydney preferred all black tight fitting clothes, no jewelry other than possible studs or rings in selected piercings, not always visible, no makeup except dark eyeliner and shadow, black lipstick and nails, and often a black leather or silk short jacket. No one should confuse her with Louise.

"You have a hairdresser?" Oscar said.

"Well, it's a salon and I can get a manicure, pedicure, facial, hair. The works. Hey, I've known her longer than you. We talk. She knows the real me. And she knows all about you."

"That sounds embarrassing. Does she know what you do?" Oscar wondered what Sydney had told her about him.

"Yes. She thinks I'm the gallery manager at the Rose Madder Gallery. A self-inflicted promotion. Anyway, I told her I didn't want anyone to know I was living with you at this point, so if anyone asked I had been staying with her and gave her the Louise info. She's had her own challenges so she's good with that. And the cops might not even ask."

The Ramirez/Hunt team was on time. Oscar didn't want to profile detectives based on popular opinion, but they looked like they were wearing the same suits and ties as before. Ramirez again took the lead once settled in Oscar's office. They handed over their cards once again.

"Thanks for seeing us Mr. Leopold. I know you're busy

so I won't take up your time."

Oscar knew that was bullshit. They would stay until they had answers to all the questions they had already asked and would get around to the new ones eventually. After going over the events of the fundraiser again, including how he was invited, how much money he contributed and who else did he know who attended, Ramirez got to the real reason he was there.

"By the way. Did you happen to arrange for Louise Nevils to talk to us?"

"As a matter of fact I did. She's in the back, waiting her turn. She's nervous though and wants me, as her attorney, to be present when you talk to her."

"She got something to hide?" Hunt opened his notepad to a fresh page.

"You know better than that. She has the right to have me here if she wants. I doubt she knows anything that can help."

"You never know what might help. Have her come in."

Oscar went back for Louise. The wig and contacts were in along with fresh pink lipstick. She whispered, "Don't get used to this," as they walked back to the office. Oscar pulled another chair up to the desk for her and introduced the two detectives.

After having her read the advice of rights card, they asked a few basic questions, including where she lived. She gave Gloria's address.

"And where do you work, Ms. Nevils?"

Louise pointed to a one-quarter size terra-cotta sculpture on a pedestal in the corner. It was a nude that Oscar had done of her a few months ago.

"That's me."

They turned to look. "So you're an artist?" Ramirez

asked.

"No. That's my body. I'm an artist's model. Not as easy as you think. Try not moving a muscle for hours on end while someone looks at every inch of your naked body and recreates it in great detail. You should endure that to see what it's like."

Ramirez laughed. "I doubt anybody wants to see me like that." Then he got down to business.

"How is it you were at this fundraiser? Do you know the judge?"

"No. Oscar asked me if I wanted to go. Not like a date, but so he didn't have to go alone. He promised good food, but there were just appetizers. And cheap wine." She looked at Oscar, who just held his hands palms up.

"But I wanted to see what it was like. I'd never been to a place like that. The only time I ever saw anybody in a tux was either at the prom or getting married. It was pretty cool. Of course we didn't know somebody was being killed nearby at the time. That was terrible."

"Did you know the victim?"

"I didn't know anybody except Oscar. But I'm out-going, so I might have talked to him. I talked party talk to a lot of the people there. But most of them were old. They didn't seem to be having that good a time." Her voice was off, Oscar noticed. Kind of lilted, a little higher pitched than normal and sing-song. She could have been an actress.

Ramirez continued questioning but got nothing out of her. Then he flipped his notebook back several pages.

"I talked to most everybody at the party," he said. "One or two remembered you. Mostly the men. One of them saw you talking to Mr. Atwood."

Sydney blushed. Oscar wondered how the hell she managed to do that. It had to be on purpose. He had never known her to be embarrassed about anything.

"It's probably my hair. Kind of flashy, but I like the red. That's why they notice me I guess."

"Is that your natural color?" Ramirez asked.

"Wouldn't you like to know?"

"Yes."

"Of course it's my natural color. I thought of dying it but my mother would kill me."

Ramirez looked down at his notes again. "And one last question. What happened to the tattoo that several people mentioned? A heart on you left arm? I don't see it."

Sydney didn't miss a beat. "Oh, that. That was just décoration. I change it all the time. I actually do have a tattoo, but it's not where you can see it. You don't have to see it do you?" She stood and started to unbutton her shorts.

Ramirez stopped her with a quick "That won't be necessary." He closed his notebook, stuck the pen in his jacket and stood. "Okay. I think we have enough for right now. We're going to check into a few things for the file. Try to be available if we need to talk again."

Oscar locked the door and they went upstairs to relax and debrief. Sydney changed and ditched the wig after confirming from the upper window that the detectives were gone.

"What if Ramirez had wanted to see your tattoo?"

"Then I would have shown him the skull and crossbones on the right cheek of my ass."

They decided to eat at home and went over the entire situation to see what might be done proactively to resolve the Luke Anger problem. He, and whomever else he might have told, were the only people who could link them to any of the killings.

He might be thinking the same thing about them.

8

The Rose Madder Gallery had posted hours, the sign read: *When the gallery lights are on, or if the door's unlocked, we're open. Otherwise by appointment or most of the time on Saturday afternoons.*

It was Saturday afternoon. Oscar was in his studio working on the latest sculpture. He had to keep busy to stop thinking about the problems they were facing. Vanessa, his model for the sculpture, had just left and he was proceeding to cut the clay sculpture apart so that he could hollow it. The idea was to remove all the wet clay possible from inside, leaving just the shell, which would then be reassembled, touched up, dried, and fired in the kiln in the back room.

The whole Pastor Luke and rose-bible deal was always there, lurking in the shadows of his mind, but he tried to work around it. Keep the brain otherwise occupied.

Sydney was in and out. She found reasons to walk through the studio while he was working with the model. Oscar didn't think Sydney liked Vanessa but thought her attitude was funny. She denied being jealous. There had been a sprinkling of visitors to the gallery, but they were lookers, not buyers. The door buzzer buzzed again, indicating another visitor. Oscar was about done, but had wet clay on his hands and needed to clean up.

"Sydney, could you check on the gallery for me?" he said as he walked to the back to the sink.

They made a point of sticking a head in the gallery when the door buzzer sounded just to let people know someone was there if help was needed. And to make sure it wasn't a neighborhood kid looking for a quick grab and run. Not that there was much in the gallery to grab that anyone could sell. If it was that easy Oscar would find out who they sold the stuff to and sell it to them himself.

Sydney walked to the front of the building, went around the corner into the gallery area and nearly bumped into the visitor. Judge Sylvia Pocholi. From the fundraiser and gallery opening. Where Louise and Sydney had met her face-to-face.

"Excuse me," they said simultaneously.

"No harm done," said the judge. "Louise, isn't it? Or is it Sydney? I thought about it and I'm sure you came to the party with Oscar. I won't even ask about the other outfits and the names. Artists do such strange things. I prefer your look now. Nice to see you again."

Sydney was flummoxed. She thought she looked totally different then than now and didn't think she had made much of an impression on the judge in the few seconds they had talked at the fundraiser. Not enough to see through the disguise. Different hair, eye color, clothing style, eye makeup, no make-up. What was up? But the woman knew, somehow, an instinctive sense. How to handle this? Deny or admit? Both?

"Sydney." She held out her hand and the judge took it. "I work with Oscar, and we sleep together. Welcome to the gallery. If there are any questions, I would be happy to assist." Sydney smiled and retreated. What the fuck? She would wait and see how the judge reacted. She reacted.

"You are so funny. No, I'm sure you said you were Louise. Different hair and such, probably party dress, but I know it's you. That aside, I would like to purchase this painting." She pointed to the largest and most expensive piece, a collage on board. "I assume I can't take it until the show ends, but I want to buy it now. It would be perfect in my office." The judge was apparently ignoring the name mix-up and was standing in front of her choice, probably imagining how it would look on her wall.

"Let me get Oscar." Sydney slid back to find him, her heart uncharacteristically thumping. She may have been found out. Well, not found out exactly but the fact that she was using two names and in disguise. Why would someone do that Pocholi might be asking herself? Could this go further? Not good. She explained the situation and Oscar took over, suggesting that she go upstairs out of sight until the judge could be dismissed.

Sydney had always taken extreme measures for security. There had been only one other incident where she was close to being discovered, when someone walked in while she was arranging an accidental drowning in a family pool. It proved hard to come up with a good explanation as to why she was holding the man's head under water. That had led to flight and a change of identity. New York to Florida. This was not as close a call as that but still, a mistake, probably caused by her need to be near Oscar. The heart ruling the head. She had to wait and see if this was a problem. It might be that the identity meld was not an issue with the judge. Nothing criminal or suspicious on the face of it except for one glaring problem. A yet-to-be-identified guest at the party may have killed Mo.

Fifteen minutes later Oscar came upstairs. Sydney went to him and hugged him tightly.

"Is it okay?"

"I think so. She didn't mention you. In fact she was kind of flirting with me. But the artist will be happy to hear I sold her piece. Don't worry. If she remembers the two of you being one at all, it will likely be written off as a girl thing. A different face for a different space."

"You clearly don't know a damned thing about girl things. I like the slogan though. But it will only be a problem if she calls Ramirez or is re-interviewed." Sydney went to the refrigerator looking for any opened or unopened bottles of wine. She took this unexpected situation seriously. For Sydney, proper planning meant there were no surprises. This was not a write-off regardless of Oscar's relaxed attitude. He was charmed by the woman all of a sudden. What happened to his previous attitude toward her?

"I should have done it differently. Not gone to the party. It was stupid."

"We didn't know for sure he would be there. Or exactly where he was staying. We needed confirmation and you got it. Relax. Nothing is wrong at this point. All the trouble we have right now is based on a few what-ifs."

Later in the day Detective Ramirez left a message on her cell. He wanted to talk again. He had been unable to pin down some of the things she had told him. Could she come into the precinct at her convenience in the next day or two? Sydney called her hairdresser. She wouldn't pick up. She jumped on her Harley and went to the salon. It was closed.

Gloria Olivares lived north of the city in a rough section of Riviera Beach. Sydney had been there a few times. It was in an old neighborhood not far from the Intracoastal. Most of the small yards had no grass and few had trees, those few being mostly shaggy volunteer cabbage palms and stands of spreading bamboo. Sydney parked in the driveway and went around to the front door. The step up into the house was only about four inches. The house, like most others in Florida, was built on a concrete slab. When a hurricane was headed her way Gloria said she stacked all her furniture and personal belongings on cement blocks to get them up off the tile floor.

A storm surge had flooded her house once before and she had learned to deal with it. She would even have her stove, refrigerator and washer/dryer elevated. She said the precaution was usually unnecessary but there was that one time she had to shovel three inches of sand out the front door after the storm surge abated and the sea water drained back out.

Gloria was home. She let Sydney in and resumed packing.

"What the hell you doing, Gloria? Taking a trip?"

"I'm going to visit my daughter in Philly until things cool down here. That cop Ramirez saw right through our cover story. He asked too many questions about you that I couldn't answer and didn't believe you lived here. I told him he was wrong and that you were just here on a night-by-night basis so didn't keep your stuff here, but he didn't seem convinced. Now he's probably going to start looking into my history and there's a couple of things I want kept right where they are. I don't want this to be my first arrest. It wasn't that fingerprint card was it?"

"No. But I wouldn't worry. He's not after you and really not even after me. Just doing his job. Investigating a case where I might have been a witness. He has to fill in all the holes." Sydney sat on the couch.

"He ain't filling no holes with me. I'm out of here for a while. Call me in a month if I'm not in custody. Sorry if I screwed things up for you." She zipped up her wheeled travel bag and stepped to the door, an invitation for Sydney to follow.

"Get back soon," Sydney said. "I don't want to have to find someone else to make me beautiful. It's a hard job and you are getting good at it." Sydney got on her bike and put the helmet on. Gloria was putting her bag in the back of her battered Honda.

"You take care. And take care of that man of yours. Ones that want to stick around are hard to find." With that Gloria left and Sydney headed back home. It was time to make decisions. She checked the voice mail for the cell number she had used for Louise. There was a message.

From detective Ramirez.

He wanted her to come into his office "voluntarily", the option being having uniformed officers pick her up. Ominous.

He didn't know who she really was or where she lived, but this was trouble. Potentially a warrant could be out for her. They probably had her down as "a person of interest". He would likely come to the gallery looking for a redhead.

Being nervous about the possibility of her cover being blown was a long forgotten feeling. She felt an adrenaline surge; a fight or flight feeling. She could hit I-95 on the Harley and be in Georgia by nightfall. Or she could try and solve the problem instead of running from it. Save both Oscar and herself. Or more correctly, save the lifestyle and comfort she was experiencing for the first time. She decided to go for the save. The simplest choice was running. But solving the problem would be most satisfying in the end. If it could be done.

9

According to the news an anonymous caller found Julie, freed her, and then identified the Mercedes license plate as having left the scene of the crime. Mary was questioned as a suspect by the police in Julie's abduction and drugging and she initially denied everything. Her new plan, she later told Luke, had been to go to Julie's bedside to be there when she awoke, then possibly to bribe her to keep her mouth shut.

Or maybe, if Julie was on life support, to unplug her. She said she had no idea Julie would be unconscious this long, but she secretly hoped for brain damage. Those plans, such as they were, went off the page when Julie regained conscious-ness before Mary's arrival. She immediately named Mary as the one who had been driving her. The police were saved a lot of trouble when Mary showed up while they were still questioning Julie. Mary had been arrested.

The first person she called was Luke. He put the church lawyers on it, arranging for bail. Luke met with his publicist, trying to find a way to mitigate the damage this might do.

"Maybe Mary was taking pills for some unrevealed history of depression or mental illness," Joan, the publicist, suggested.

"She wasn't depressed," Luke said.

"We have to spin the story to keep you and the church above it all. You could release a statement, expressing your sorrow and concern and let it slip that, while it hadn't been announced yet, Julie would be receiving the full boat scholarship from the church to Baylor University in Texas."

"Yes. That might work." Luke thought that perhaps that would buy Julie off. He was hoping the lawyers would arrange to let him bring Mary home where she could be sequestered until this all was resolved. No one had yet put forth a theory as to why the pastor's wife would drug and kidnap a young girl. At least Julie hadn't told them her phony rape story. Yet.

The weekend was coming up and he had made no preparations for his sermon. He would have to rehash another old one. Maybe use the teleprompter this time. The last choice, and maybe what he should do, was use a rerun of an old show for the radio and television feeds and have one of the assistant pastors take over the sermon in the church. The staff would handle it. That's why he paid them. It would be understandable that he had to spend time with his wife. He was not ready to make an on-air statement about the situation with Mary and Julie. Congregations forgive, he wasn't worried about that.

"You know it occurs to me that the free publicity of a scandal would bring even more viewers to your show. Lemonade from lemons," Joan said. "The networks might even pick it up. Maybe we could swing a reality show out of this."

The recording studio sat directly behind the altar area of the church auditorium. The auditorium itself had padded chairs, more like the old movie theaters rather than bare wooden pews. At the rear of the auditorium was a platform for a television camera and another was normally also placed at the right side of the room, covering the choir and a side view of the sermon. The operations center was the studio, where Mary normally worked with her staff directing the camera shots and supervising the feeds. It was all computer controlled and state-of-the-art.

There was a sound-proof recording room behind glass adjacent to the control room that was used to make the recordings for Christmas and Easter albums and downloads for sale online. There was even a catalog of selected sermons arranged by topic. All these could also be downloaded to one's favorite electronic device—for a fee of course.

Luke would work with the attorneys and staff on damage control. Keep Mary out of public view. Away from even the congregation. Maybe send her to an out-of-state spa for therapy or some such. That would play well with the public to show she's voluntarily getting help. It seemed to work for the Hollywood stars when they got into embarrassing situations. Go to rehab, get out of trouble.

This whole situation had to be resolved once and for all. His life was on hold and he felt that everything he had worked for was slipping away. Mary had become a serious liability. Plus there was the problem with Julie. Luke was surprised at Mary's foolish actions. Mary had thought the girl a danger and had taken steps to neutralize her but hadn't thought things through. She was usually very methodical about serious decisions.

She should have discussed it with him and they could have solved the problem together. Now they were potentially in trouble. The kidnapping and drugging of Julie was a serious criminal offense, but that was mostly Mary's problem, not his. He thought he could survive the publicity by pinning it all on his pathetic wife. He had more important things to do right now; deal with the killings and find his hired killer.

10

Sydney was stowing packets of cash in her backpack when Oscar checked on her. She was near her computer desk with the bag on her chair. She looked up but continued to pack the money.

"I know what you're going to say. Where did you get all that money? Well, I earned it. This is part of our retirement fund. If I don't come back, more of it's in the bathroom. What you do is open the medicine cabinet, remove the two screws inside that are holding the cabinet to the wall, pull the cabinet out, mirror and all, and you will find a cavity inside under a false panel with a canvas bag full of cash. It's yours."

"I thought everything went through foreign accounts."

"It does. But I have an ATM card for each account that allows me to withdraw up to five hundred dollars a day each. So that's what I did for a while until I had this war chest filled. I also have a stack of one-ounce Canadian gold coins buried out back under the closest orange tree."

"What I was going to ask is where are we going?"

"Me, not we. Things are closing in on me, Oscar." She stopped packing and stood with her hands in the bag, looking for his eyes.

"Ramirez checked out Louise's story and it didn't pass. The judge knows that Louise and I are one and the same. Then my banker contacted me through my secure line and said there were inquiries being made about my closed account in Venezuela through Interpol—probably instigated by the FBI. May or may not be related. It's like a tightening noose. The signs are bad and there are too many of them. If I can't solve this situation right away I have to be ready to close down the Sydney-Louise operation."

"How about the Oscar-Sydney operation?" He went to her and she hugged him tightly, her cheek to his chest.

"I'm not through with you any time soon. You're the only pal I've got. They aren't targeting you. Plus you're a lawyer. They're going to be very careful. They already have something on me they can prosecute." She leaned against the table facing him.

"You mean lying to a police officer? Impeding an investigation? That's not much."

"It's enough to arrest me. Then they can start digging. Why do I have two identities? That's probably a crime. Where did I come from? Why have I never filed a tax return? One thing can lead to another. Plus my prints would be put into the system. I can't have that. It's time to go. You have to stay for a while. Take care of the gallery. You have the cars. The dog. And somebody has to water my bonsai." Her eyes were glassy, but no tears spilled.

"To hell with the cars, the bonsai, and the gallery. I'll put them and Jesse under the care of Angelo and his boys down the alley. I'm going with you. In fact this might turn out to be the best thing. We'll be free to do nothing but solve this case."

"What case? We are already ninety-nine percent sure that Pastor Luke killed the boy and set us up to make it look like a serial killing. There's no murder to solve."

"But the bad guy is still on the loose. We need to prove that he did it and make the cops think he's likely responsible for the others as well. They have no evidence on either you or me on the deaths of Earl, Mo, or the fishmonger. We're going to make them look hard at Luke instead of looking for us. Let's take a little vacation and spend the time putting Luke away."

She thought for a long minute. "Okay."

The packing now took a different turn. They would

leave the Harley and the Mustangs. Sydney had several other identities that had their own credit cards and they used one to rent a Chevy Suburban, like those used by the Secret Service. She had a wide array of tools and equipment that might be needed. They took the money, computers, disposable cell phones, various weapons and different types of clothing. A portable cooler carried water and sandwiches.

They locked up and left the keys and Jesse with Angelo along with Jesse's favorite toys and a fifty-pound bag of dog food. Instructions were on the desk of the gallery for the gallery volunteers and they left for their "vacation". The cops didn't offer the standard television advice of "don't leave town without telling me", so they were off, with, at this point, no wants or warrants out on them.

"If this plan doesn't work, we're going to have to change identities and relocate." Sydney said as they got into the car.

"No problem. I go where you go."

They were pulling away from the building when Sydney stopped them.

"Wait! One more thing." She ran back to the building and went inside. Oscar assumed a final bathroom break, but she came out a minute later holding a bonsai. She put it on the rear seat and buckled it in.

"I'm only taking the one. This was my first and I can't bear to leave it."

"Whatever makes you happy. Is it going to need a new identity? I'll change its name for you." He pulled out into traffic.

"That's not funny. If it turns out we have to disappear, you need to understand how it works, Oscar. It's not as easy as you think. It's like witness protection except you have no one to rely on except yourself—and me of course. Once we decide to leave we pick up Jesse and the rest of the money, and then can't ever come back here. No calling Roy or your family except on very secure lines from locations remote from where you actually end up living. I can get you a new name and papers and we have cash. That's usually the biggest problem. But we have to have a good cover story. Keep out of the public eye. Even after ten years, there's no running for treasurer of the country club or getting your picture in the paper for that hole-in-one. We're off the grid permanently."

"How about another country?" Oscar said.

"You have to be careful where you go if you try that. In most countries you need a visa. A lot of the officials are corrupt and a foreigner stands out. The government will sometimes steal your money or blackmail you. Remember Robert Vesco back in the 80's?"

"Yeah. What I read in law school was that he stole two hundred million from his company then fled the country, eventually settling in Cuba where he couldn't be extradited. He ended up in a Cuban jail with his money seized.

"So we're better off to go to a larger city in the continental U.S. far away from here. Small towns are like foreign countries too in that a stranger is noticed and people speculate about him or her. We need to be in Seattle, San Francisco, or LA. Maybe live on a boat, claim to be artists."

"Easy. I'm already an artist. How about New York?"

"I already burned that bridge. I just want you to know what you might get into. We will have to live modestly and not attract attention. And if something happens to me you have to keep up the ruse. They could get you as an accessory after the fact. Harboring a fugitive."

"Hey, I'm the lawyer. I know the crimes I've already committed. Those others would just be add-ons. Throw-outs in a plea bargain. Most of the things they might have on us would go away in a few years anyway. Statute of limitations."

"Except for murder."

"Yeah. There's that."

"It's just that you don't have to go. I can disappear and your troubles go with me."

"And so does my life." Oscar kept his eyes on the road.

Sydney looked over at him.

"Don't be so melodramatic."

11

They went back to Orlando, this time renting from a non-chain hotel with an outside entrance, ground-level where they could park outside the door. Sydney talked the desk clerk into letting her leave the bonsai in the lobby window. Better light, she explained to him and Oscar. She knew it seemed silly but it was somehow important. A way of grounding herself. Sydney had her own mobile internet access so would not be using the motel WIFI. She had already assembled all the information she could from the news media about the killing of Jerry Prado.

First it was reported as an accident. Then after the autopsy as a possible homicide—a sex act gone wrong. Then when the roses and bibles became evident in the other murders it was lumped in with the others as a serial killing and the investigation was taken over by a multi-jurisdictional task force.

Oscar pulled all the information he could from Roy's law firm case files on the church and on the Pastor. While the settlements with victims of Roy's child molestation cases were private, one had been handled by Roy's firm, where Oscar was now of-counsel, and he got a copy of the internal documents. He read them over and gave Sydney the highlights.

"This guy should have been arrested in this case and two previous ones. He must have some heavy clout. Three cases of sexual assault on minors, two girls and a boy. All were paid off and the families then moved away and dropped out of the church."

Sydney was sitting in front of her computer at the small desk in the motel room. "Were they forcible rape?"

"He claimed consensual, but look at the facts. A fortyish man, authority figure, has private sessions with these kids, almost adult bodies but still children mentally. He talks them into sex. Gets them used to the idea by watching porn movies with them. Feeds them alcohol. Who knows what kind of line he feeds them. Maybe they're intimidated, too scared to say no. That's from the file. To me, that's forcible. But it doesn't matter how it happened. Sex with a minor is a felony, the same as if he had dragged them into the weeds. Pisses me off that he can buy his way out of this kind of crap."

"So we think the Prado boy was another sex-toy for the beloved pastor and somehow he killed him. Then tried to make it look like a suicide."

"Yeah. He probably remembered the rose and bible and planned all along to plant them on other bodies to draw the investigation away from him." Oscar said.

"Where it surely would have eventually led."

"Right. The local police may look the other way and wink at the sex stuff, but not murder. His ass was on the line."

"Pretty smart. And the thing is, it's still working. We need to get some evidence that he killed Jerry Prado so that the police start searching in the right direction. I've been thinking about Jerry's father, Clint Prado and his suicide. Jerry spent occasional weekends there lately according to his mother. He had to have his own space. He may have left things there. I think we need to check out the scene of the suicide."

"We haven't heard that the police have released the scene yet."

"We can get the address and already have a legitimate reason to be there. If we get caught we'll claim a misunderstanding. It might tell us something that no one else has stumbled on."

"Why wouldn't the cops have looked into it already?" Oscar said.

"Clint killed himself after Jerry's death. They probably

did talk to Clint before he died, but wouldn't have any reason to do a deep search of his house if it looked like a suicide. We have got to take a look."

Clint's house was located in an aging subdivision of two-bedroom ranch houses just off the entrance ramp to Interstate Four. The lawns were brown and mottled with sand and grass clumps. The houses sat far back off the road. No trees were in the yards. Clint's mailbox was missing but the house number was on the front door. There was an unpainted plywood wheelchair ramp at the front and a shell driveway led behind the house. They could see the police tape and seal on the door when they drove in.

Sydney had no trouble entering the locked rear door. They parked the Suburban behind the house and had seen no neighbors outside when they drove through. The August heat kept everyone inside in the middle of the day. In the house there was no question as to where the death scene was located.

"Those gray organic specks on the ceiling are more than likely brain tissue." Sydney lay back on Clint's narrow bed, her hands clasped behind her head. There was no pillow and no blanket. Just a sheet she had thrown over the bare mattress. She could feel the crinkly feeling of the pool of dried black blood that had soaked into it. Oscar was appalled.

"How can you lie there? That's just creepy." He went into the dining room to sort through papers in Clint's roll-top desk.

How had he felt, she wondered? What had he thought when he lay in this spot day after week after month after year, unable to walk, his life in ruins? The headboard and ceiling were splattered with dried blood and brain tissue now. There was a hole in the headboard that continued through the wall. The rifle shot that killed him. Sydney looked through it and saw the light of the outdoors. He was paraplegic. Did he have a housekeeper?

The room had an unpleasant odor when they first arrived. Open windows had cleared much of it but it was still there. Oscar didn't smell it at all.

"How can you not smell that? Ugh."

"I have found," Oscar said. "That having a poor sense of smell is a blessing. When I could smell things the odors I remember were mostly unpleasant."

"You mean like autumn leaves, a freshly cut orange, the perfume behind my ears?"

"No. Rotting food, unbathed street people, the oyster beds at low tide, seeping septic tanks—things like that."

"What if the house was on fire? You wouldn't even know."

"That's why I've got you, babe."

Sydney thought that Clint would not have been able to get out of bed as easily as she could. The wheelchair was still within arm's reach and she pulled herself into it, not using her legs. Clint had none. It was not one of those electric power chairs, just a cheap fold-up with a canvas seat that would fit in a car's trunk. She rolled out of the bedroom following the clean trail the police, or maybe the coroner, had made with the nearby upright vacuum, clearing away brain matter and blood from the thin carpet. A visible path through the dried gore. She wondered if they had changed the bag or if it was still full of Clint.

Out the door of the bedroom and to the left down the hall was the single bathroom. Inside, chrome rails followed the walls into the tub and beside the toilet to facilitate him getting around in there. She left the chair in the hall to use the bathroom which was remarkably clean compared to the carnage in the bedroom. The tub, though small, was shiny white, clearly new and was fitted with little Jacuzzi jets. Everything else, the tile, light fixture, toilet and sink looked original and shabby. Probably mid-sixties, featuring avocado-green, popular at the time she had heard.

Straight ahead down the hall was a tiny eat-in kitchen with one window over the sink looking out into the yard and a doorway which stepped down to two doors: the basement to the left and outside to the driveway to the right. There were only three chairs at the table. Clint must have stayed in his wheelchair to dine. She could see the top of the Suburban through the kitchen window. It occurred to her that Clint couldn't see out the window from his wheelchair and could not have used the kitchen door because of the steps but had to use the front one with the ramp.

The refrigerator was empty save for a half-bottle of vodka—not the good stuff—and what was left of a bucket of petrified Colonel Sanders. In the vegetable drawer there was a plastic bag of what she recognized as dried psilocybin mushrooms looking like gnarled gremlin buttons and another small packet of white powder that she tasted and knew was cocaine. Her urban street education providing the identi-fications. Why hadn't the police confiscated them? Did they even bother searching the house?

She stood at the sink staring out the window. An old Chevy van with a flat front tire squatted in front of the one-car garage, looking like a lame elephant. She could see it was the kind with a wheelchair lift built into the side. The weeds in the yard could use mowing and she wondered how Clint had managed that. A lawn service? But the place was too unkempt for that kind of organization. Probably neighborhood kids looking for occasional work.

Clint's desk was on one side of the living room and

Sydney rolled up to it as Oscar was going through the paperwork from the drawers.

"The detective was right as to Clint's character—the guy was an outlaw—but he was probably not right about the suicide theory."

"What did you find?"

"Well, the death was caused by a single rifle shot under the chin which blew out the top of his head and exited through the outside wall. But how he had pulled the trigger? His rifle was an old Springfield 30.06 with a thirty-inch barrel according the paperwork on it that I found. Clint couldn't have reached the trigger with his hands and still get the barrel under his chin and pull the trigger as he had no feet or toes. Not a suicide."

"Thing is, maybe nobody cared if an outlaw got offed. He was a bad guy who had bad habits and worse friends. Bad guy dead, case closed."

"That's what I'm thinking."

The other documents gave some information on Clint's life. The Orange County Tax Collector showed ownership of the van in the driveway as well as a fishing boat and a three-wheel motorcycle, neither of which were on the property. There was one bank account with direct deposit of his disability check and a balance of three thousand seven hundred thirteen dollars. No insurance except for the policy provided by the Veterans Administration. There was nothing else. No big deposits or withdrawals, but drug people dealt in cash, so that was indicative of nothing.

"Jerry supposedly spent every other weekend here. So where's his stuff?" Sydney said. "You, know, the extra clothes, maybe music, or books. Where did he sleep? There's no boy's room here. The second bedroom is full of junk piled to the ceiling. Can't even get the wheelchair in there."

"What do you think about the basement?"

"Yeah, the basement. Unusual to even find one in Florida. That would give him privacy since Dad couldn't get down the stairs. Teenagers would like that."

They checked. The stairs off the kitchen would have been a formidable problem to Clint. They turned on the lights, single bulbs at the top and bottom of the stairway provided feeble illumination to the dungeon-like hole.

The basement floor was unfinished concrete. To the left was a littered area surrounding an air-handler for the air conditioning and a hot-water heater. The ceiling was open to the floor joists above with pipes and wiring running every which way. To the right was what must have been Jerry's space. It was like an efficiency apartment. Sydney pulled a string attached to a fluorescent fixture on the ceiling and it was much brighter. Jerry had a table with books, magazines, and photos scattered on it. There were disassembled models of what might be airplanes if assembled. Small jars of paint and glue. A straight-backed chair matching the three in the kitchen. The single unmade bed was against the back wall.

There were several posters of what must be current music idols, one poster larger than the others that Jerry had modified by drawing a mustache on the female singer.

Sydney and Oscar were both ten years past knowing what teenagers were interested in or who the posters represented. An old style non-flat-screen television was to the right, visible from the bed and had a cable box on top of it. There was no computer, no cell phone, no letters or diary. But it was messy. No organization. Typical or not? It was no help.

Everything seemed to be just like it was left before Clint died, or was killed, or committed suicide. Whatever, he was dead no matter how you called it. They left, not realizing what they had discovered, and returned to the motel.

12

"I think another visit to Luke's office would be in order," Sydney said.

"Do you think that's wise? We've been there once and didn't leave on good terms. Plus, what if they've found the bug?"

"It quit transmitting a few days ago. There was hardly anything on it. And how often do you look at the bottom of a table? Or even know what it was if you found it? But I was thinking of making an after-hours visit. Check his desk. Maybe there's a safe behind a picture like in the movies. See if there's a laptop or photos or anything we can use. Guys like him keep trophies. Underwear or videos. It wouldn't be at his house where the wife could find them. The office is his man-cave. That's where to look. Don't worry, I can get us in and no one will know we were there; except him if I take something with me and he finds it missing."

They made the preparations for the visit later that night.

"I'll wake you at three if you want some sleep." Sydney said.

"Why so late? I'm thinking ten or eleven this evening."

"Three or four in the morning is when the cops bust down the door to serve their arrest warrants on the perps they're after. The bad guys are asleep and disoriented when they wake up like that, plus the neighbors are in the same situation and there's less likelihood of outside interference. Did you know that if you are awakened suddenly your small motor skills are impaired for a while? Hard to grab a gun and aim it when you're like that. And nobody stays that late at work. There are damn few people awake at that time of the morning. If it works for them it works for me."

They stayed up, getting their gear together after having coffee and a late snack from the all-night convenience store down the street. She brought out night-vision goggles for both of them and equipped her mini-helicopter model with infrared video. They changed into dark clothing. Each carried a small handgun, though they didn't expect any use of force would be called for, but self-defense was always a possibility with Luke, the loose cannon wheeling around.

"Should be a quick in and out," Sydney said as they surveilled the church on foot from the vacant land at its rear. They had climbed the chain link fence two hundred yards down from the gate and worked their way toward the church building. It was hard going and Oscar complained of getting scratched up by the palmettos. Sydney worried about the snakes that she hoped were dormant at night.

They watched the building for a half-hour from just off the parking lot area. There was no gate guard, the gates were closed and so far no security had shown.

"Did you bring insect spray?" Oscar kept slapping himself on the face and arms.

"I'm one of those people that mosquitoes don't bite. You must be sweeter than me."

"I hate people like you," he said as he slapped again. "There might not be any security at all. It's a church, not a bank. The compound is fenced in and we're not close to any urban centers. No reason to do much more than lock the door. Probably not much to steal anyway."

"I didn't see any security cameras when we were inside last time. Just fire and smoke alarms. There might be a burglar alarm, but I didn't see one. No motion detectors or window sensors. This could be an easy job after all."

"Famous last words. Don't jinx us."

Sydney set up the miniature helicopter. It was state of the art, really a drone, operated by remote control with a thousand-foot range. It could be bought unmodified online or at most retail stores for less than one hundred dollars. The on-board camera transmitted a video signal to her IPod. It was electric and totally silent. She started it and it lifted off and hovered in front of them. She pushed forward on the controls and it took off toward the church.

Oscar watched it until it disappeared in the darkness, then it reappeared as a moving dot as it got near the outside lights of the parking area behind the church building. The video was good until it picked up the parking lot lights, then the screen blanked out. Sydney switched off the infrared and the video came back on. The helicopter moved upward, then circled the building. There was nothing to see, no cars, no people. It came back around and went up to the big windows in Luke's second floor office. She switched to infrared and let it hover. The office was empty. The window shades were up and there were no lights on. Sydney brought the copter back and put it away.

"Okay. Good to go." She said.

They pulled the infrared goggles back on and picked their way through fifty more yards of palmetto brush to the parking lot at the back of the building.

"Do you think snakes are awake at night?" Sydney said as she plowed through the brush. "I read about those giant Burmese pythons that they say are big enough to eat you."

"Maybe you, you're not that big, but not me. No. Those are further south toward the Everglades and in the swamp. What we have here are mostly big rattlesnakes and copperheads. Stay away from standing water too; that's where the water moccasins hang out and they're pretty aggressive."

"That's all a comfort. But good pickings for the pastor's

Sunday performances I imagine."

There was a steel door at the rear for the employee and service entrance. Sydney was pulling out her automatic lock pick when Oscar tried the door. It was unlocked.

"These churchgoers are so trusting. Don't you just love them?" he said.

"They're pretty confident of their big gate, I guess."

They stepped inside. They were both all in black, even to the rubber gloves. They had entered what looked like a lunch room for staff. There were dining tables, chairs, and a counter with a sink, microwave, and a small refrigerator. They padded across the tile floor, out the door into a hallway, and found their way to the stairs leading to Luke's private office. All the lights were off but the night vision guided them clearly.

Upstairs they entered the office and began searching. Sydney brought a gym bag to carry any items they might find and she set it on the desk, then began going through the drawers. There was an oak horizontal file cabinet to one side of the room and while it didn't look promising as a hiding place Oscar sorted through the files anyway.

Sydney pulled back a floor rug and called out softly.

"Take a look at this. A safe." She went to her bag and pulled out a stethoscope, then took nearly ten minutes to get the safe open. "Got it."

"I was beginning to doubt you."

"Look what I found." She was holding up a handful of photos. With the goggles on and the greenish light Oscar couldn't tell what she had.

"Child porn," She said. "Not nice. No pictures of him, but lots of his victims in all states of undress. Some show parts of what is probably his body, but taken by him, so no face shots of him. God!" She tossed them on the desk. Oscar leafed through them quickly. There were fifteen, likely taken with a digital camera and printed in color on his office all-in-one printer, no doubt, since it was on the credenza behind his desk. The backgrounds were not all familiar, some were outside, others in bedrooms and only one in the office on the couch near the bookshelves. Lots of crotch shots. But there was the one that struck them both.

The picture had no faces showing and they had both originally skipped past it. Just a photo of two male sets of genitalia. But in the background was a poster on the wall behind the bed. The same large poster that had been in Jerry's basement room at his father's house. The one with the mustache.

"Have you ever said Eureka?" Oscar said. "This is some good evidence. Not conclusive of anything except Luke was in Jerry's room in a sexual situation. Not so good for Luke."

"And not for Jerry either."

"Is it possible, do you think, that Luke killed Clint? Maybe Clint found out what was going on and had to be eliminated."

"Why didn't Luke stage this as a rose-bible murder then?" Sydney said.

"Too close to home. He couldn't have father and son done by the serial killer. It would invite too much scrutiny. What we really need is to pressure Luke into confessing. I know that only happens in the movies, but it would certainly help."

"I have an idea," Sydney said, taking the pictures from him. "Let's scan these and copy them to his computer. Then I'll save them on a flash drive and delete the scans. That way, we have some ammunition and if the police should happen to seize his computer, forensics will be able to pull up the deleted pictures from the hard drive. Even without the prints the picture files will be recoverable."

"And what? Get him on possession of child pornography? We need to prove he's a murderer."

"Take what you can get as far as evidence and we'll build it from there." She opened Luke's laptop and used the printer to scan the pictures to a file, then transferred them to her flash drive and deleted the picture file. While she was in the computer she copied his emails and all Word document files to look at later. She punched the computer up to reveal hidden files, but there were none.

Sydney pulled the rest of the stuff from the floor safe. She hesitated, then decided to take the several bundles of hundreds so if he discovered the break-in it would look like a robbery. She also found the envelope with the information about her and her website. This was in the safe so she was hoping it was the only copy and kept the contents, putting the empty envelope back.

They had been there twenty minutes, more time than they had planned. They slipped out the back, retrieved the toy helicopter, struggled through the underbrush, and made it to the car.

It was five in the morning by the time they got back to the motel and they did nothing but strip off the ninja costumes and sleep until noon. Oscar went out for coffee and carryout for lunch while Sydney examined the computer files she had copied. There was a folder labeled *Private Counseling* that she thought would be pay dirt, but it read more like a psychologist's case notes.

She read through them. It didn't seem that Luke had much to offer in the way of help. His notes restated what the kids told him about their problems at school, with parents, and with the other students. She found Julie's file but there was nothing interesting in there either. What they had in common, she realized, after reading a half-dozen, was the blank pages at the end of each file.

She had an idea. The guy couldn't be that stupid, she thought, but maybe he was. She highlighted the last page of a file and clicked the font color key. He thought he was hiding his notes by coloring the text white, so a casual look would reveal a blank page. She changed the white text to black and the page filled in with the hidden paragraphs. Now she had something to look at. It was a summary of the sex acts he had engaged in with Julie and what promises he had made. A scholarship, maybe cash and a car. Other files for other victims detailed specific sex acts and such things as a trip to a sports event, cash, cell phones, computer games. Little gifts and comments about what Luke liked best about each victim. There were dates listed as well. It was a confession. But of sexual assault, not murder.

Sydney turned to the Jerry Prado file. A full account of what happened when he died. Including Luke's belief that he had been responsible for the boy's death.

Bingo and Eureka again.

13

Luke's feeble attempt at hiding his notes was curious to Sydney and Oscar.

"He didn't even have his computer password-protected, and the door to the church was unlocked." Sydney said. "Now we easily find the hidden text that puts him directly in the police headlights. Maybe he wanted to be caught. Or he was being set up. His guilt might have subconsciously made him careless."

"Or maybe he's so arrogant that getting caught didn't seem like a possibility. A God complex. See—I can be a psychologist too."

Oscar had finished reading the Jerry Prado notes. The whole pathetic incident was laid out in detail right up to the time Luke abandoned the scene, not even calling 911. Oscar was relieved there was no mention of Luke contacting Sydney's website.

"This is good stuff, but not enough to convict him," Oscar said.

"What do you mean? It's a confession for God's sake. And we have pictures of him and Jerry. It seems like enough to me."

"If I were defending him I'd say there was no proof Luke wrote those notes. It could have been his wife or a staff member to frame him. I would perhaps admit the sex, but deny the murder. Jerry could have been doing similar things with any number of people. At least that would be the defense. They still have to prove guilt beyond a reasonable doubt, regardless of how awful the crime. And your copies of the notes and pictures were illegally obtained and inadmissible. We need to tip off the cops and send them some pictures so they can do their own search and discovery."

"We can't do that yet," Sydney said. "We have to prove the murder if we plan on getting out of this ourselves. Putting him in jail on rape or child molestation would be a good thing, but won't help us. The books won't be closed on the other deaths until Luke is charged with at least one of the murders. They will more than likely stop investigating then, convinced they got their guy. There's a lot of public pressure to solve this case."

"What we have going for us is that Luke overestimates himself." Oscar filled his coffee cup. Sydney leaned back in her chair, her hands clasped behind her head, looking at nothing.

"Suppose we confront Luke, in private, in his own space where he feels in charge? He would be comfortable there and might admit more than if he were arrested. No lawyers to advise him. We could show him the pictures. Tell him we know everything. Make it look like a demand for blackmail—something he would understand."

"Why would he meet with us?" Oscar said. "We can't very well call for an appointment and say we want to discuss his role in the rapes and murders. And why talk to us anyway? He knows I'm a lawyer. He wouldn't do it."

"We don't ask. We tell. He might think he's in trouble with the Julie sex situation. She hasn't gone public on him yet. His wife is facing a hit for drugging and abducting the girl, but who knows how that will come out? I think Luke would like to keep her silenced. It would make sense to meet with you if you implied you were working for her and he could buy her silence. Everyone would want discretion. A private meeting off the books that we record."

"I have an idea. How about if we send him, via email maybe, one of his treasured pictures. Then say we want to meet to find a way to keep it quiet. He will surely know this is for real and not some phony shake-down. He has to meet and on our terms."

"That's a good approach. Copy me a picture I can upload and I'll send the email and then let's see if we can meet up with him alone this evening," Oscar said.

"Let's make it tomorrow night. Saturday. I need to go back there tonight and lay some groundwork to get things set up first. We want this meeting memorialized on video. I have a good idea how to end this whole thing. Let's find out where the nearest computer store and Radio Shack are located. I need supplies and a little time to write some code."

14

The tools and equipment Sydney needed had been acquired and she spent the day assembling her components and working at the computer. They waited until evening and went to the church grounds.

The front gates were closed, it was raining in squalls and lightning flashed intermittently.

"I don't much feel like climbing that fence again and picking my way through the underbrush in this weather. I don't want to be the tallest thing in that field when lightning comes to visit." Oscar had stopped on the side of the road a hundred yards from the Temple entrance.

"Okay. Then let's drive up to the church with the lights off. I'll open the gate for us if you pop the trunk."

"Do you have the combination to the key pad in there? Or some other fancy high tech piece of equipment I don't know about?"

"Strictly low tech this time."

Sydney got out, fumbled around in the trunk and came back to the driver's side door with the car's jack and lug wrench. She had put on a ball cap to keep the rain off her face and wore a short black cape which shed the water. Oscar rolled down his window.

"I know you're resourceful, but do you think we can just jack the gate up and slide the car under?"

"You maybe don't know how these gates work. Go on ahead and pull up to the exit gate. I can't get in the entrance side easily but the exit is pretty simple. To get in from the entrance side you have to have the pass code or use the intercom and someone in the church will use a remote control to open the entrance gate. Good security to keep the unwanted out. But once inside, it's assumed you're there with permission. So the exit gate opens automatically when a car approaches it."

"You mean like in the supermarket." Lightning cracked nearby followed by the thunder boom.

"No. That's a motion detector. Can't use that on a gate or every loose raccoon, falling palm frond, or armadillo would set it off. Exit gates use what amounts to a magnetic relay embedded in the pavement. The steel in a car or motorcycle sets it off as it passes over. So we're going to trick it. But you have to drive in as soon as it opens since there's usually only thirty seconds or so and it shuts again." Oscar stayed in the car watching through the headlight glare and rain as she crouched down and slid the lug wrench under the gate with a hard push. It rolled, skidded and stopped.

The gate didn't move. She looked back at Oscar, smiled, and gave him a thumbs-up; though he didn't see any progress. Then she took the larger steel scissor-jack and repeated the push. The jack travelled straighter, about two car-lengths, stopped, and the gate clanked into motion. She walked inside, picked up the hardware, and got back into the car after Oscar drove through. They drove around to the back. The parking lot was empty except for six golf carts under a canopy.

She took the helicopter out of the trunk, turned it on and set it on the hood of the car and brought the remote control with her. This time the rear door was locked, but Sydney was in quickly. They strode quickly up the stairs to the office. They had earlier bought a duplicate of Luke's laptop, and now Sydney connected a cable between it and the original and transferred everything to the new clone, which she left on his desk, putting the original in her bag. Then she led the way to the control room of the recording studio.

Oscar stood lookout while Sydney sat at the computer console that controlled the video and satellite feeds. She plugged a flash drive into a USB port and downloaded her data. Then removed the cover from the audio-visual console and hooked up a feed of her own that she could control from her laptop. Now she could access the church intercom to send and receive audio.

She then went to the main worship area and placed a sealed envelope on the shelf under the lectern. She made some further tests and then shut it down. They left after running the helicopter around the perimeter to be certain the way was clear. It struggled a bit in the rain but made it back. The exit gate opened and closed for them.

"Now we can operate everything from outside the church tomorrow. We don't have to see him in person. We can talk to him, see him and listen, but he can only hear us. And we can turn on his satellite feed if we like or just record what goes on." Sydney said.

"So you know programming too? What else don't I know about you?"

"That's part of the fun of having a girlfriend like me, isn't it?"

Back to base the motel lot was quiet and only six other cars were there. Light showed around the edges of the draperies in a few of the rooms. The motel had a sign on the front desk, "No Pets" but two cats sat on the window ledge in one of the rooms on the window side of the draperies, looking out. The night was muggy. This time of year nightly temperatures were still in the low eighties and the humidity was nearly one hundred percent.

Sydney peeked through the motel office window to check on her bonsai. Her little ficus tree had some new tiny leaves. It would have to be watered today. The office was dark and closed but the parking lot lights lit the window enough to see. She sat on the bench outside the office and watched as the occasional car passed.

Would they get out of this mess and keep the good life going? Or would the future be another place, new people? At least she now had Oscar with her who was ready to go wherever necessary. For the first time in her life she was not a loner. Someone cared whether she came home at night. He would worry if he didn't hear from her for more than a day at a time, even when she wasn't on a mission. Her concern had always been that someone like Oscar could be a liability.

If you loved someone others could hurt you or manipulate you by threatening to take that person away. So she had shied from relationships that lasted. She had never told Matthew, her presumed dead husband what she really did for a living. She hadn't been as trusting in that relationship. It began and ended too quickly. Oscar was the only person to whom she had revealed her true mission in life—bringing justice to those the system had failed. Corny? Yes. Superhero stuff—but very real in her small way.

She was rethinking all that now. Had she done enough? The world had too many problems for one person to solve. Could she be a regular citizen? Have children? Join the PTA? How about all those people that had family gatherings for holidays? She had never done that. Thanksgiving and Christmas for her were typically celebrated at Denny's and maybe at a movie—alone. No presents to give or receive. In fact she didn't remember ever getting a Christmas present as an adult until she met Oscar.

Oscar had even been sweet enough to ask the date of her birthday and got her a package. A necklace with a small diamond studded gold motorcycle charm. She loved it.

She went back to the room. Oscar had already fallen asleep. He snored softly. She didn't mind. It was nearly morning and streaks of light were forming in the eastern sky. They would sleep until eleven or so then prepare for the day. Tomorrow was unknown. They could be free, back in West Palm resuming their lives, or on the road to wherever it took them.

15

The appointment with the blackmailer was at six. Luke had insisted on a private meeting after seeing the photo that the blackmailer had sent. Luke wanted to know how much it would take to make the problem go away, but the guy put him off, using one of his silly disguised voices, saying they would discuss the conditions at the meeting. He knew it was a blackmail situation, but insisted on seeing who the blackmailer was and what he actually knew.

He went to his safe to see how much cash he had on hand.

None.

The money and pictures were gone. That must be how the blackmailer had gotten the picture they had sent. He didn't panic outwardly. The thing to do was damage control. The missing pictures would look like child porn but someone had stolen them and they couldn't prove they were his. Probably the extortionist was the thief and the blackmail attempt was a crime of opportunity. But the simplest explanation was usually the correct one. This was the work of the hired killer wanting more money.

To be safe he took his laptop downstairs, out to the parking lot, across the field, and tossed it into a dark murky pond. His cell phone had once gotten wet and wouldn't work anymore so he assumed the same would be true of the laptop if they ever found it. Now there was no evidence. No way that he could be connected with the photos.

But maybe it wasn't just the killer's attempt at black-mail. It was possible this was a setup to murder him. He had to take precautions.

There were church activities all day Saturday and Luke

went through the motions but was completely distracted. Nancy Prado wanted to see him again. He met with her briefly and asked her to put a snake in a bag under the podium in the auditorium—for a private prayer session. She wanted to meet with him privately—it was very important, she said, but he put her off. Told her to come by later. He had one priority and it was the late afternoon meeting. The snakes would intimidate the blackmailer. Luke had no intention of going to some remote location and had insisted on meeting the guy here, in his environment.

None of the kind of stuff that had happened in Sebastian would happen again. It would be on his terms this time. He decided on keeping the blackmailer out of the office. Make him say what he had to say in the open auditorium. And Mary was around, so there would be a witness if the killer tried anything. After the staff left Luke set the lights so they pointed at the lectern where he would be in the spotlight. The blackmailer—or killer—as the case may be, would have to talk from a step below, in front of the altar. Luke knew he was an intimidating and respectable figure standing at the pulpit.

His physical size and arrogance had allowed him early on to bully his classmates in school and dominate nearly any situation he had been in since. Let the blackmailer try and accuse him in his own church. Odds were good the guy would take a small payoff if he showed up at all. Mary had stopped by and he explained he was just going to rehearse the sermon once more, even though it was a rerun. She just said her usual "hmm" and retreated to her office.

Mary had been staying closer to him than usual since the police incident. She didn't want to agree to the rehab idea and Luke had to calm her by explaining it was only if Julie refused to change her story. His people were trying to get word to Julie that good things could happen if she no longer remembered what happened when she was kidnapped. Who knew if that plan would work? Of course Mary wasn't so upset that she forgot to confirm that her skim from the weekly receipts were transferred to her private account.

16

The appointed time of six o'clock came and went. No blackmailer. No killer. The guy must have chickened out. Not likely, but Luke waited, somewhat relieved but still nervous. Three cars pulled in over the next half hour, but none came to the church. Probably some school activity, Luke thought. He finally went back into the main church area when he thought he heard someone talking. The room was empty. The lectern was still spotlighted. He heard a voice. It was coming through the church public address system and reverberated through the big room.

"Pastor Anger, I assume?" the voice said.

Luke spun and scanned the room. Maybe someone had gotten hold of one of the cordless mikes. He went to the lectern. Both were still there.

"Who is that? Where are you?" Luke said to the empty room.

"This is your friend with the information that we discussed. I want you to reach under the lectern and open the large envelope you will find there on the shelf."

Luke found the envelope and ripped it open.

He sorted through the photos on top of the pile quickly and blanched. They had come from the safe. But his picture was not in any of them. Just the pictures of his lovely children. Because he was the photographer. One child, Jerry, now sadly gone.

He tossed them and they scattered on the low carpet at his feet. "Don't show me this trash! This is a church. What is it you want? You said that somehow I was implicated in something. I agreed to meet with you to avoid slander on the church's good name. Now what is it? And show yourself. This is not what we agreed. Where are you hiding?"

"Did you see all the things in the envelope? There is more than just pictures. The other documents will be of great interest to the police."

He bent to the floor and picked up the scattered papers. In addition to the photos there were printed documents. He sorted through them. They were printouts of his notes on each victim, with the white, formerly invisible text, now printed in bright red.

Luke read each one, gradually beginning to shake as he quickly read one after another. They had been in his computer. But he had destroyed it. How did the guy have these? His eyes misted over. He shredded the pages violently into pieces so small he could no longer tear them. Then he looked up from the pile of torn confetti-like remains.

"How much do you want? Not that these mean any-thing. Anyone could have written them."

"I have the information I just showed you, several copies, in fact. But that's not why I'm talking to you. Did you see the one marked number seven? That particular one will hang you—well this is Florida and generally they use lethal injection when administering the death penalty. But the point is the same. That is the one that shows you with a naked Jerry in his room at his father Clint's house. Both are now dead as you know. You killed them.

"I think that after you killed Jerry, maybe accidentally, maybe not, but still it was felony murder and Clint was suspicious. He managed somehow to get downstairs to Jerry's space. Probably sitting down, going one step at a time, using his hands to bump his way down. He found something. Probably other photos, or notes. Then he threatened you.

"You had no choice but to come for him. Shot him with

his own rifle and tried to make it look like a suicide. This was all at about the same time you were setting these statewide killings up to look like serial killings. And they were. You were the killer. You were at the fundraiser where Mo was killed. You were there when Red the fish seller was stabbed. I imagine you won't have an alibi for the time and place of Earl the cannibal's death either. You had to have killed them all to cover up your crime."

"You're speculating. You can't prove anything. I was at those places, sure, but that doesn't mean anything. I had reasons."

"Circumstantial evidence of murder. Most of it. But Clint's crime scene is the only one still pretty much untouched. I would bet that a good CSI team could find your DNA somewhere in his bedroom where he was shot. Maybe on the rifle itself."

"I didn't kill him. I swear to the almighty. And Jerry was an accident. I didn't kill him intentionally. It was a game he wanted to play. It's just that he was so frail. Please believe me. And I didn't kill Clint. That wasn't me. He killed himself the police said. I'm not a murderer. I paid someone, probably you, to kill those other two. That cannibal monster and the conman Mo. I didn't do it myself. I am not the evil person you are making me out to be. You are the evil one and will burn in hell."

"I don't believe you and neither will the jury. You caused others suffering trying to protect your wealth and reputation. You lied and bribed and had people killed." The killer was using the Darth Vader voice now. It rumbled loudly through the church.

"I employ a lot of people. They depend on me. I loved my children. None of them were hurt except the accident with Jerry. They love me, I know. I am a man of God. I believe in the power the Lord has given me. The Lord Jesus protects me and watches over me."

Luke bent down and pulled a heavy burlap bag from under the pulpit, holding it in one hand and reaching inside with the other. He pulled out a writhing six-foot rattler, holding it in the middle of its body so both ends moved back and forth, its muscular body almost horizontal to the floor, the head with fangs exposed waving as if looking for a target. It's tongue flicked the air, sensing. The snake at its mid-point was as big around as Luke's wrist.

"Behold, I give unto you power to tread on serpents and scorpions, and over all the power of the enemy: and nothing shall by any means hurt you.' So sayeth the Lord in Luke 10:19." Luke had his eyes tightly shut.

"You are a child molester, murderer, user, and rapist." The voice said.

Luke now held the snake with both hands. It was heavy and he lowered it, the head coming closer to his body and swaying but not striking. He began preaching again. *"Thou shall not be afraid of the terror by night, nor of the arrow that flies by day, nor of the pestilence that walks in darkness, nor of the destruction that lays waste at noonday'. The word of the Lord in Psalms."* He opened his eyes, his nostrils flared and his voice thundered. "I am not afraid!"

A familiar voice rang out, but not through the speakers.

"You are to blame just as I thought. My son will be avenged."

Nancy came walking down the aisle on the path she had travelled many times before to confess herself as a sinner and seek forgiveness. This time she was there for vengeance. She carried only her shoulder strap purse and stopped just below the lectern, looking up at Luke.

"I know what happened, Pastor. I know how you perverted my son. Made him do vile things. Clint told me.

"Gerald was still alive when I found him where you left him, unconscious in his bed, naked, covered in your obscene filth. I put him the rest of the way to sleep. I knew he would not want to live with what he had done. He was tainted. From you. I prayed over him. Covered his body. Tried to clean things up. Clint would do nothing to help me. He knew what had been going on. Jerry confided in him but he did nothing to stop you. I pleaded with him but he was a worthless sinner. I had to kill him too as God surely wanted."

"Nancy," Luke began, but she overrode him.

"Gerald was just a boy. He would have done none of those horrible things if you had not perverted him and Clint had stepped in as a father should. I have been praying for guidance ever since then, deciding what to do. I waited all day here, wanting to see you. I almost went home but there is only one way that Jerry will rest in peace and that is if his death is completely avenged."

"Avenged? What does that mean? Are you planning on killing me? Right here in God's house? And you have the nerve to accuse me? You are the murderer. You killed Jerry and Clint." Luke held the snake above the lectern, his arms stiff, his face flushed and his jaws clenched. He shook the snake at her and its head whipped back and forth, seeking a target.

A voice came from the back of the altar, near the curtain next to the choir area.

"Just shut up Luke. You are a pathetic idiot." Mary stepped forward and stood a few feet to the left of him. She held a small handgun at her side, unnoticed until she raised it and pointed it directly at Nancy's chest. They were only ten feet apart.

"Mary, honey, what is this?" Luke said. She ignored him, but smiled slightly.

"A surprise," the voice said through the speakers. "It looks like even you didn't know everything, Pastor Luke."

"No. I had to clean up his mess," Mary said, looking around for the source of the voice. "He would have ruined us before I was ready to move with my plan. I'm leaving with enough money for many years to come. Luke can stay here and run his little church. It won't be anything without me. I arranged things to cover up his crimes but he's screwed that up too. He was going to get rid of Julie, maybe even kill her so she wouldn't tell about his penchant for raping children. I can't have Nancy screwing things up so I'll take care of her too. And you," she looked around the vast room as if to see where the voice originated, "I'll be long gone before whoever you are can find me. I've made arrangements."

"You helped plant the roses?" said the voice.

"Luke had already left the rose and bible at Jerry's place. It seemed like a good signature. He told me about hiring some hit man to kill those other two so I stayed close and went to the sites with him. I insisted on going to the fundraiser. Good riddance I thought. Probably not even a sin to take their lives. But I knew when the killings were likely to take place and took the roses and bibles with me. We were able to place them at the scenes to make his plan work. If it turned out the hit man didn't actually kill them there we would have placed them somewhere else. Nothing lost." Mary beamed, as if she had just won an award.

Luke held the snake to his chest, his mouth open but no words coming out. His eyes were wide as he stared at Nancy, then turned to Mary. The rattlers neck curled back, lifted its broad head with its mouth opened wide exposing the inch long fangs and then struck him twice in quick succession in the shoulder and neck. He dropped the serpent and collapsed.

"The anti-venom," he said hoarsely.

Mary went to him, forgetting Nancy and the gun she had been pointing at her.

"I have it," Nancy said, pulling from her bag a vial and syringe and holding them out.

"Bring it here, quickly!" Mary said. Luke was jerking and writhing on the floor in a full blown seizure.

Nancy went forward, filled the syringe from a glass vial, and injected Luke directly in a vein.

Luke stiffened. He was still breathing but his eyes were closed and he was drooling.

"Give him more," Mary demanded. The two women were crouching over Luke's body.

"Gladly," Nancy said. She injected him again. He shuddered and lay still. The trousers of his white suit darkened with urine.

"What happened? The injections didn't work." Mary grabbed Nancy's blouse with her free hand, shaking her.

"They worked fine. I've been saving the venom I milk from the snakes. I seem to have forgotten to remove the venom from this one as well. I just put three doses straight into his bloodstream. My son has justice." Nancy grinned.

"No!" Mary lifted her revolver and shot Nancy in the chest. She fell backwards over Luke's body. The sound of her head hitting the floor echoed in the cavernous church. Nancy stood, the gun hanging loosely at her side. She looked at Luke and Nancy, tears ran down her cheeks, the gun slipped from her hand and she fled, running toward the back door of the church.

17

Oscar and Sydney were stunned. It had happened in seconds. They were in the Suburban at the back of the large parking lot and could have tried to intervene but it was useless. There was no need to attempt CPR on either of them. Sydney sent a command from her cell phone to shut off the television feed. The Mercedes careened around from the back of the church heading toward the gate.

They drove up to the front door slipped into the worship area. The smell of cordite and urine was in the air. Sydney confirmed that Luke and Nancy were indeed both dead. They went up to the office and dropped off the pastor's laptop after seeing that the clone was no longer on his desk. The rattler was nowhere to be seen. They left slowly in the Suburban, Sydney driving this time.

"How soon before the police arrive?" Oscar asked.

"Probably on their way right now. The cameras were on during the whole show thanks to my programming. The audio and video has already been sent off to all the television affiliates. I would expect some of the stations did a little preview while it was feeding in. The police should be here in no time at all. The confessions are all there. The pastor and Nancy laid it all out."

"It's funny. We were all wrong about who killed Jerry. Luke wasn't a killer after all."

"But he thought he was. That's what precipitated this whole mess."

"Now it's over and we're in the clear," Sydney said.

"Should we call 911?"

"We have a dozen television and radio stations doing

that for us right now."

18

They stayed at the motel for two more days, watching the news and checking their phone and email messages. Run or return home? CNN was featuring the story. The video was available in so many venues it had leaked and the entire scene, including the killings was available on the internet. Television showed the confessions and the snake bite but skipped the shooting; although a few stations played the audio, including the gunshot.

There was live coverage of the police arresting Mary Anger. She was to be arraigned on multiple counts of murder and would likely be facing the death penalty. Her trial would keep tabloid television busy for months.

To see if there was any unpublished information they stopped back at Roy's Orlando office and talked to Juanita Ortega. They commiserated, terrible thing that happened etcetera, and Juanita gave them a few details not available on the news.

"Luckily for us, the church had big insurance coverage so our lawsuits are going forward."

"The bus case, you mean," Oscar said.

"Yes. And how did your investigation go? Are you going to be able to proceed with your case?" she asked.

"No. We had interviewed the pastor, with his lawyers, and they threw us out of the office not very politely. With the pastor dead I plan on closing that file," Oscar said.

"They're still looking for the mystery voice that appeared in the broadcast. Any idea who that might be?" Juanita said.

"No. Do they need that info?"

"I don't think so. Of course they like to tie up all loose ends, but the video speaks for itself, and I heard the photos and Pastor Anger's computer pretty well wrapped up the case for the task force. Six deaths. Amazing what people will do to protect their stuff."

"Stuff? You mean their power as well as the money it brought?"

"Yes, all that. It also seems that there was a large amount of cash in Mary Anger's many different company accounts. That will likely go back to the church, or whoever takes it over. After expenses of course," Juanita said.

"You mean like attorney fees and investigative costs."

"That's the way the game works."

On the way home they stopped at the Valkeria Bonsai Gardens and Oscar tried to be interested as Sydney picked out enough new bonsai plants to fill half the back of the Suburban. The gallery was dark when they arrived. Oscar held her hand as they walked down the alley to pick up Jesse who had been staying with Angelo. It was early evening, the heat of the day was dissipating and they shuffled through fallen schefflera leaves littering the unpaved alley.

"Are you still worried about getting caught?" Sydney asked.

"No. I think it's pretty well wrapped up. And actually I think it would be difficult to get enough evidence to convict either of us for anything."

"You didn't actually do anything illegal you know," Sydney said.

"Aiding and abetting and accessory to murders. Acting as a getaway driver and lookout. Breaking and entering. Larceny from a building. That's enough. But no, I'm not worried. I have other things on my mind. Like you. I was wondering about your marriage. Who did the ceremony?"

"It was very new-age. Kind of like the bonsai guy. The minister ran a commune that was on its last legs in the Poconos. I even had flowers in my hair believe it or not. Pretty relaxed and romantic."

"Where did you get your marriage license?"

"I remember we signed a form the guru guy gave us. It had a gold seal and there was a poem on it he said he wrote. I don't know what happened to it—probably Matthew kept it."

"Where did you sign the form? At the county clerk or courthouse?"

"No. It was informal, like I said. Listen, I was young, had never gotten married before and didn't know the procedure. Still don't. It seemed correct at the time."

"So it's possible you weren't legally married at all. Probably weren't. That makes things simpler."

Sydney stopped and turned to him. "Really?"

"Really. And not that it makes much difference, but what exactly is your real name anyway? We're going to need it for the new license one of these days."

"To you Oscar, it will always be Sydney."

She held his arm with both of hers, leaned her head against his shoulder and they walked on.

END

Author's note:

Thanks to the folks at Poisoned Pen Press for starting this series with the first book, No Regrets, No Remorse. This is a work of fiction and all the characters of course are fictitious. Those who are familiar with Florida may recognize that I have changed the descriptions of some places and even made up others. I can do that because this is fiction. Special thanks to my agent Sarah D'Emic for her help with the manuscript and the valuable editing and plot advice from Tarah Ash, Elise Troczynski and Susannah.

About the author

Ronald Farrington Sharp won the Poisoned Pen Press Discover Mystery Award for the first Sydney Simone book in this series, *No Regrets, No Remorse*. He has won awards for his short stories and is the author of two non-fiction self-help books. A former attorney and lifelong sculptor, his artworks appear in dozens of galleries, collections, and public spaces. He lives on land in Ann Arbor, Michigan and on the water surrounding Florida with the artist Susannah Keith.

www.ingramcontent.com/pod-product-compliance
Lightning Source LLC
Chambersburg PA
CBHW022036240626
47154CB00007B/2434